## RARE GEMS SERIES BOOK 6

# KATHI S. BARTON

**World Castle Publishing, LLC**
Pensacola, Florida
Copyright © Kathi S. Barton 2015
Hardback ISBN: 9781629893136
Print ISBN: 9781629893143
eBook ISBN: 9781629893150
First Edition World Castle Publishing, LLC, August 7, 2015
http://www.worldcastlepublishing.com
**Licensing Notes**
Cover: Karen Fuller
Editor: Eric Johnston
Editor: Maxine Bringenberg

# Chapter 1

"If you taught her better, we'd not be having this problem."

Emerald looked at the paper in front of her and counted to ten. It was that or hit the asshole in front of her. She hated parent/teacher conferences almost as much as she did balancing her checkbook. Smiling, she looked up at him.

"Mr. Basel, I've sent home numerous notes about Shayla's reading issues. She is behind all the other children by fifteen percent. She is to read a chapter a night, and–"

"I don't have time to do your job. And if she has homework to do, then tell her to do it. I'm not taking the fall for your incompetence. If she fails, then I'm going to come in here and kick your ass." He leaned back in his seat as if to say, "What are you going to do now," and Emerald had to count to twenty this time. "If you can't do your job, then maybe they should find someone that can."

"You're absolutely right. You can do it." She stood up and so did he. But the difference was, he looked panicky and she was not. "The school board will expect you to be here at seven, even though classes don't start until nine. You have to do your own room clean-up at night...budget cuts, you know...and then there is the bathroom. It would be better for you if you clean it the night before you leave. The stains are as hard to—"

"What the fuck are you talking about? This is your job." She shook her head and started stuffing things into her bag. "You're not going anywhere. This is your job. And I'm not gonna take it."

"You'll have to. As I see it, you've just fired me." She stuffed another book in her bag and looked around for anything else she might be able to take. Everything in here was basically hers. The school she was working for this summer had no money and very little resources. "There is the matter of supplies. I'll take all that is mine, so you'll need to pick up some chalk, erasers, and some pens. I'll leave you the paper. I can't use that anyway."

"Now see here." She moved toward the door, only to be blocked by him. "You can't just pick up and leave. You have to teach them kids. My daughter will try...what do you mean, this stuff is all yours? My taxes pay for this stuff."

"No, it does not. You voted down the tax levy for the school, and that is the reason you can't keep full-time teachers, especially in the summer. The little money you pay in taxes is for the upkeep of this place, which, I must say, isn't working out too well. There is nothing left for the classrooms, much less for the teachers. I purchase the toilet paper they use, paper towels we need, and any other things that you might not send along with your child." She glanced down at the sheet in front of her. "Oh, sorry, you didn't pay your fees, which means that everything your daughter is getting to use — tissues, notebooks and pencils, and paper for art time — is coming out of my pocket."

"No, that ain't right." She just stared at him and then stepped around him. "I pay my taxes. That should pay enough.

"Well, it doesn't." She moved into the hall and found nine more parents in line to talk to her. And for the most part, none that she really had to speak to about their kids. "I'm sorry, but Mr. Basel will be taking over for me. He just fired me."

"Fired you?" Everyone turned to the man coming out of her classroom, and one lady continued, "You fired her? How the...do you have any idea how much she's helped my son? He's reading now when no one else could get him to do that before. What the hell do you think is gonna happen to him now?"

"I didn't fire her. It was just a misunderstanding. Come on back, Ms. Erickson, and I'll talk to you about my little girl. Perhaps she can...I'll make sure she reads two chapters a night to catch up." She turned to look at him. "Please? I've had a rough couple of days. I lost my job. I'm raising her on my own."

"I don't need this crap, Mr. Basel. I'm a good teacher." Several of the other parents nodded and glared at him. "I'm here because this district is out of money. My time here is mine. The little bit of money I'm making to help your student get ready for the new school year is less than half what I make elsewhere."

"I didn't know that." She didn't say anything. It was so tempting to go home...to simply say fuck it and lay on the deck chair by the pool at home. But Mr. Basel continued before she could make good on her wants. "We didn't know a lot of stuff about this place. Did you all know she has to clean the bathrooms and pay for all her own chalk?"

Several of the parents looked shocked. Others were pulling out their wallets. Emerald felt stupid. She should never have said any of those things to him. It was just...it was true, but wrong to whine to him. Emerald refused the money that was pushed at her.

"I'm sorry, too. I should never have said those things." One of the parents asked if she really had to clean the bathrooms, and she nodded. "The custodian was let go due to budget cuts. We either do it or it doesn't get done. But that doesn't mean that I should have said that to him. I'm not having such a good day either."

"But that's not right." Emerald couldn't have agreed more. "You should have some help. Where is the help? I thought the schools had previsions for this sort of stuff. Volunteers and stuff."

"Very few signed up for it. Did you volunteer to help me out this summer?" No one would look at her. "I'm sure that a paper was sent home. If even one of you came in one hour a week to help out, so much more would be done. Someone could sit and have a child read to them for that hour and it would help. Helping on projects, art, or other things would help out. But no one, not a single parent, signed up to come in at all."

"We can't just leave our jobs to come here and not get paid." Mr. Basel turned away when she looked at him. "I guess we could make a little time. Even if I had to, you know, leave early. But I don't have a job right now, so…well, maybe I can come in and help out."

"And I would love it." He nodded. "There is only so much we can do for these kids on our own. You have to do some of it at home. Have them read to you while you're making dinner. Have them read the labels at the store, tell you the prices of things. Even have them tell you what time it is. All of these things take very little time out of your equally busy days."

Emerald went back into her classroom and sat down. She wouldn't leave the district in a bind like this. After about twenty minutes of sitting there alone, she figured that they'd all gone home. She was putting her things back on the desk when the parents, all of them, came into her room. Emerald wanted to sob, they all looked so upset with her.

"I'm terribly sorry. You have every right to be upset with me. I should never have said those things to you, nor should I have threatened to quit. I'm so sorry." Mr. Basel shook his head. "If you call the board in the morning, they'll tell you that I've given my notice. This was—"

"Christ, don't do that." She stepped back when he shouted at her. "I mean, please don't do that. We were…well, I was wrong to talk to you that way. We've been talking and it seems that none of us have been all that helpful to you at all. None of the teachers, as a matter of fact."

She sat down when he did. The rest followed. "I'm not even a part of this district, but I'm sure there are a lot of them like this one. On the verge of closing down."

"We got that. Some of us…Charlie here is gonna come in after he gets off work in the morning and clean up the rooms. Millie is going to make sure that the bathroom is clean on her way home from her job." Emerald started to speak, but he cut her off by standing up again. "Now you listen here. We already have this worked out and you're gonna do what we say for a change. Mark there is going to work on the school yard stuff. He said he noticed that some of them swings are in poor shape. He'll get some of his buddies to help you out. Here."

He shoved an envelope at her, and she was afraid it was cash, but it was written on and she read down the list. They were coming in and this was the schedule. Tears pooled in her eyes, and Emerald had to wipe them twice before she could look at them.

"This will help so much." Two of the women nodded and told her they'd bring in snacks when they came in too. "I don't know what to say."

Mr. Basel laughed and looked around the room before speaking. "That would be the first time since I met her. She ain't done nothing but jabber on since I came in tonight."

Embarrassed, she smiled at him. "I'm really sorry about that. I've had a rough day as well. Seems some students have taken it into their head to be artists in my classroom."

She got up and let the map that was at least fifty years old slide up on the roller. She was so embarrassed to let them see what the "artists" thought of her naked, but it was there and they all had a right to know. She turned to look at them when no one said anything.

"I don't know who did it. It's paint, so I have to have someone come in and take care of it for me. I'm not able to...well, I've been trying to deal with this, and it might have gotten the better of me." She pulled the map back down. "I have been conducting interviews about it, and no one knows a thing."

"You let us take care of that too." Millie Shaw stood up. "I got me an idea who might have done that, or at least the ring leader, and I'll have a talk with his momma. You see that I don't. Shameful the way kids act today."

"You don't have to do that." She only nodded and sat back down. "I'm overwhelmed by this. I can't thank you enough for the support you've shown me tonight."

It wouldn't last though. Emerald wasn't so naive that she thought they'd do as they said. It was summer after all. But when they left, they each said they'd help all they could and would talk to the other parents as well. Emerald nodded. Mr. Basel was the last to leave.

"Shayla will read tonight and every night. I promise you. She's been slacking on her other grades too. Too much phone time, I'm thinking." She said nothing, as she'd had to take his daughter's phone from her several times these past two weeks. "With me out of a job, there won't be a phone for her to play on anyway."

"Call my brother-in-law, Josh Ewing. He's looking for some laborers. I'm not sure what they're doing, but perhaps they might have something for you." He nodded and turned to look at her as he made his way to the door. "Thank you, Mr. Basel. You've made my night."

"Shouldn't have messed it up for you." He nodded toward the map. "I'll be in tomorrow to get that off the wall for you. I know a few tricks."

She nodded and led him out of the building. The guard was there and locked up when she told him that she was finished for the night. Going back to get her things, she wondered if she'd have anyone next week to help out with everything. There were all kinds of things going on then, and she could really use the help. The testing for the state was all the board seemed to be focusing on anymore, and she was worried about the kids that were struggling.

~~~

Jul Whitney's head was pounding, and he thought perhaps he might be having a nervous breakdown too. This was the day…hell, it was the week from hell, and he wasn't sure how much more of it he could take. Glancing at his desk calendar, he groaned. It was only Tuesday. What the hell was he going to do with the rest of the week?

"You should know that there are five more men coming in today. And none of them are as qualified for the job as they think they are." Jul glared at his assistant, Colby Bass. "I told you not to run an ad in the paper. You should have hired a firm to find someone to replace Mr. Williams if you really need to have a partner. This is not the way to go."

Daniel Williams had been his partner up until nine months ago. But he'd decided that life, his life, was not what he wanted flashing before his eyes when he passed from this world to the next. It was boring, he'd told Jul, and he wanted something exciting.

He'd had a massive heart attack, and was lucky to have been visiting his daughter at the hospital when it had happened or he'd be dead. Now he was giving up the business, selling out, and going to retire to parts as yet unknown. And Jul was going to have to replace him.

"Why?" He looked at Colby. "Why are you even looking for someone to come in and take half of what you make? Unless you like giving away your money. Do you?

But I know you can do this. You did it the entire time Mr. Williams was in the hospital, didn't you?"

"That was different." Colby asked him how. "Because I knew he was coming back to help out. Besides, what do I do for a vacation should I want one?"

"I wouldn't know. The five years I've been here, you've never taken one. Nor have you taken any time off, so far as I can see." Colby stood up and smiled at him. "You're just simply a workaholic. And while that's wonderful when you want to buy whatever you want because your bank account is bigger than the national debt, you can't meet a woman and settle down if you work all the time."

"You're what, twenty-five, twenty-six? What do you know about settling down and having a woman?" Colby took out his phone and shuffled around on it before handing it to him. The woman there was beautiful, as were the three children, two boys and a little girl.

"I'm thirty-one. Been married to my high school sweetheart, Dawn, for the past twelve years, and we have three children as of now. Best thing that has ever happened to me." He took back the phone and looked at the picture. "Yes, sir, the best thing that can happen to anyone."

"I don't think I'm cut out to be a husband for anyone. I'm too...set in my ways." Colby nodded. "You know, you could have disagreed just a little. I mean, I am your boss, you know. But you're right, I do work too much. And get me whatever information you have on me going solo on this business and I'll look it over."

"It's on your computer. I uploaded it yesterday. Look under 'Get rich all by yourself.' That should help you a great deal." Jul opened the file and looked up at Colby.

"You should be my partner." Colby shook his head and shivered. "Too much for you? Well, I got news for you...I can't run this without you."

"You're right, you couldn't, but that doesn't mean that I want to be a partner with you. You're a very good businessman, smart, articulate, and you have an amazing sixth sense about wine and food, but you work too hard, and I'd have to try and keep up with you. And I won't do that." Jul understood and nodded. "Besides, who would set up your meetings and keep you sane?"

"No one like you can."

Colby thanked him and left him. Jul knew that if there were any more interviews today, Colby would cancel them. He was deep in the file, making notes and writing out questions, when his mom walked in the room. If she knocked, which she seldom did, he didn't hear her.

"I've been out talking with that young man of yours. I think he's right, you should just run this alone." He leaned back in his chair and smiled at her. "You're doing a bang-up job now. And what's to say you won't be better at it?"

"Dan was Dad's partner. They ran this company before me here in the states and back in France where the winery is. I don't know what to do on my own." Which was a lie. He'd just read notes indicating that he knew just what he was doing. "What if I fucked up and lost it all?"

"You have more money than you can spend in five lifetimes. A house on every continent in the world. Credit cards for those things you don't have cash for, which would thrill me to no end if you'd spend some of it on yourself." He grinned at her. "I got the deed this morning. Why on earth would you buy such a thing for me?"

"Because I love you. And you said you wanted it. It's a lovely house. I stayed there last summer when I was in France for business." She nodded and smiled at him. "When do you leave?"

"Later tonight. But not directly to the house. There's a friend of mine I'm going to go and see. I just found her on that social network I've been playing on. Her son and daughter-in-law were killed some time back and she raised their children. Six lovely girls. Imagine that."

"I'm not getting married so you can have grandchildren." She huffed at him. "Besides, you can go and play with hers and you won't have to worry about dirty diapers."

"I'd love to change a dirty diaper of one of my grandchildren. And to set the record straight, she has great grandchildren. You remember her, Annabelle Erickson." Vaguely. He nodded, frowning. "You remember her son, then. He played ball at the high school when you were just in grade school. Your father loved taking you to those games."

"I remember that. I never met the guy before." She nodded as if she knew that. "Why are you going there now? I thought you would have left this morning to get the place in order. Is she ill or something?"

"No. She's just someone from my past, the past I had with your father, and I want to see her. She's excited about me coming for a bit, and I am too." Jul nodded and wondered what was really going on. His mom was a wonderful person, but she rarely did anything without having an ace up her sleeve. "You should come with me."

"I can't. I'm going to...I've decided not to take on a partner and to run this place on my own, as you and Colby have suggested." Her smile lit up the room. "I'm not sure I can do it. I might have to get a partner later on."

"You'll do better than your father did. I know it. He had a good head on his shoulders too, but you shine with it. If this business hasn't doubled its income by six months, then you're not trying as hard as you should." She went to the door. "It's only three now. I should be there by ten tonight. I've left the information to where I'm going with Colby. Should you need me or want to come and see me, I'll be there for about a week. I want to catch up. I'm headed straight to the airport now and should be there in about an hour."

"Have a good time, Mom. I'll see you when you get back." She stared at him for several seconds before turning and leaving him. Jul wanted to call her back and ask her why it was so important for him to go with her, but he didn't. Instead, he opened up his file again and started reading.

It was nearly midnight when he left his office. He'd made the decision to keep the business his own about nine-thirty, and began making some calls overseas to see if the grapes and other things that he needed to make their product was on line to get a production here in the United States going soon. He wanted it close to home as well as in France. But here, he wanted to start something new.

It was the plan he'd proposed to Dan some years ago...to produce not only the best wine and champagnes in the world, but anything else that would be eaten with them. They had a line of crackers and cheeses now that sold as well as, and in some places better than, any of their single wines. He was very proud of that. But he wanted to bring that part of the business here to the States. It was something that he and Dan had been talking about before he'd gotten ill.

Jul was on his way to his car when he felt something jab him in the back

"Give over your wallet." Jul turned to see what the person had said to him when he told him to stand still. "Just give me the wallet and nobody gets hurt."

"You're not going to believe this, but I don't have a wallet. No cash either." He laughed quietly. "As for you thinking no one is going to get hurt, you're wrong about that. I plan to beat the living shit out of you as soon as I turn around."

"I have a gun." Jul laughed again, and the man poked him in the back. "Do you feel that fucker? I have a gun."

"Nah, a hair brush. I thought at first you might just be using your finger, but that's too big for that. It's your hair brush, or your mom's." The man hit him in the back with something hard. "Yep, hairbrush."

The shot rang out, and Jul felt pain in his left side. He didn't think about that as he turned quickly and popped the gunman/would-be robber in the face with his briefcase. Then when he was going down, Jul kicked him in the head hard enough to shove him back against the pillar that was holding up the floors above.

The man didn't move, and Jul's had a sudden wave of dizziness as he noticed the gun still curled in the guy's fingers. Christ, it was fucking big. Pulling out his cell phone as he kicked the gun away, he called the police, then the front gate. He had no idea how the guy had gotten in, but now that he was here, he was going to be dealt with. After the guard told him he'd let the police in, Jul called his mom.

"I've been shot. I didn't want you to read about it in the papers and worry." She asked him what he was doing calling her and not going to the hospital. "I'm waiting on the police. They'll have to deal with him."

His head spun, and he had to grab onto something or fall. His mom was talking, but he had no idea what she was saying to him. Just as he started to notice that the floor was becoming extremely close to him, he heard the siren getting closer. Jul dropped the phone as his mom was screaming something about murdering him when she got there.

"I'm sorry," he said just as the lights in his mind shut out.

# Chapter 2

Annabelle sat on the big plane and listened to her old friend Celeste Whitney talk about her son. It had been decided as soon as they found out that her son had been hurt that Annabelle would go back with her. Somehow Annabelle was shoved onto Blair's plane along with Celeste, and they were flying back to where her son was being operated on. When Celeste paused for a moment, Annabelle asked her what had happened.

"I'm not sure. He called to tell me he'd been shot. Just like that. 'Mom, I've been shot and don't want you to see it in the papers.' As if that would make it any better for me hearing about it from him." Annabelle had to hide a smile. Celeste was really upset. "Do you have any idea how terrifying that is?"

"I do. My granddaughters are forever getting banged up about something or another. Their husbands aren't much better." Celeste smiled at her, but it was watery. "At least he could talk to you. That has to be something."

"Yes it was. That very nice policeman said that he was taken to surgery as soon as he got to the hospital. That was over an hour ago. I hope he's out by now." Annabelle nodded. "He's all I have now. I want to make sure he's safe, but this kind of stuff happens all the time in that city. I really hate it there sometimes."

"My youngest granddaughter, Emerald, works at a private school, and someone held their student's captive for hours on end before someone went in and got them." Annabelle didn't mention that her other granddaughter had gone in and gotten the kids, or that she'd been hurt doing it. "Things happen in all sort of towns, big or small."

"I suppose. But my Julius was killed there, and I'm forever wanting Jul to move the business to somewhere less violent. I know that there are madmen everywhere, just as you said, but in a smaller town he'd have less of them to worry about." Annabelle could relate to that. Their last pack had been horrible, and it was in a larger area. The pack was small, but the alpha was a menace.

As soon as they landed, they were escorted to the hospital by a limo that Blair had arranged for them. Annabelle wasn't overly fond of the long car, but she did noticed that Celeste seemed to be used to it. As soon as they made it to the hospital and up to the floor her son was on, Annabelle reached out to Sapphire.

*We're here.* Sapphire told her she was glad they'd made it safely. *I still don't know why I'm here. This is her family. I have green beans to pick and put up. Not to mention there are cherries that won't pit themselves.*

*Allen picked the green beans this morning and got some of the pack to come in and fix the cherries. We're going to simply put them into the freezer until you return.* Annabelle was glad for that. Not that they needed the food her garden put out, but it was very relaxing for her to do. And she loved Allen, Blair's father, helping her do it. Sapphire spoke before she could ask her about the tomatoes. *You're there because you've not had any time to yourself since we moved here. And you've been looking forward to her visit for weeks now. She needed a friend, and you were there for her. Did you see the way she clung to you when you told her you'd go back with her?*

*Temporary insanity.* Sapphire laughed. *Her son is out of surgery. She's visiting with him now. Poor boy, she wants him to move to a smaller town so he won't get hurt again. I had no idea that her husband was killed there too. I'd have moved you children to a safer place too if I'd had the means.*

*You took care of us. And we'll be forever grateful for you and what you gave up to keep us all together.* Annabelle told her that they were her grandchildren and she'd never leave them to others to raise. *That is the reason we all love you with every breath we take.*

Ten minutes went by before Celeste came out of the room. Annabelle thought they were leaving, but her friend insisted that she come see her boy. Annabelle hated to intrude but went anyway. The young man looked a good deal like his father.

"You're Mrs. Erickson." Annabelle nodded. "My mother is silly for coming back here. I told her that I was fine. She didn't have to cut her visit short."

"Nonsense. I would have done the same thing for any of my family as well. And when you have one, you too will go no matter what they tell you." He flushed and Annabelle had to smile. "You look just like your father did at this age. And my goodness, he loved your mother. I remember the first time I saw them together, I thought to myself 'there is a match made for the times.' You should have seen them together."

"They didn't get any different as I got older, either. My dad would bring her roses just because he could. And once, when I was about fourteen, he took her on a trip to see fireflies in the Smokey Mountains because they'd seen it on the news." Annabelle nodded at him. "I do hope you're not leaving soon. Mom was really looking forward to seeing you. She'll try to say she needs to care for me, but I'm fine. Seriously."

"You should come with her then." He was shaking his head. "No, listen to me. You want her to have a good time, and the only way she's going to do that is if she knows you're all right. What better way than if you're just down the hall from her?"

"I can't do that. I'm trying to get my business running after my partner left me. There just isn't any time. Not right now." Annabelle nodded and stood up. "You understand that a man has to work."

"I do. More than you can know. But my husband said that nearly every day of our lives together. *Tomorrow* was his favorite time. I loved him dearly, but he...." She looked around the room to gather her wits for a moment. "He had a son that missed him terribly because he needed to work every day. Then one day, he was gone from our lives and there were no more tomorrows to promise on. Then when my own son and his lovely wife had to take a long business trip, I watched their six daughters for them so that they could enjoy some time together while they worked. Neither of them returned. There are no tomorrows for them either.

What will you do, young man, when there are no more tomorrows for you and your mother?"

Annabelle left him then and walked down the hall to reach out to her granddaughter, Sapphire, again to tell her that she was coming home tonight. But she reached for Emerald instead. She could feel her sadness almost from the moment she touched her.

*I've lost my apartment. I knew that they were going to go to condos, but we were told we'd have first options in buying in. What they didn't tell us was that we'd have to pay fifty thousand dollars to do so. I never looked around for something else.* Annabelle started to tell her that she could move back in now, but Emerald started talking. *I'm not moving home again. I just can't. All those happy couples there all the time. And before you ask, yes, I'm jealous. I'll never have that.*

*You can have it.* But Emerald said no. *Why not? Why can't you have what your sisters have? You're a beautiful young woman and have a great deal to offer someone.*

*Grandmother, I'm a school teacher with no money, and no prospects of ever having any. I don't want a husband that will want me to take care of him. The rest of them have been so lucky in that their husbands are rich and love them so much. But what do you think the chances are that I'm going to find the same kind of man? None. Zip. And I'm not sure I want a mate that is so rich that he forgets what a homegrown tomato tastes like.*

Annabelle smiled at her comment. Just before she'd left, a man that seemed to irritate Emerald more than most did had come by the house. He'd scoffed at the idea of growing your own vegetables and had even made fun of Emerald when she'd told him that she had a garden in her back yard too.

"Why? Don't they have them at the store where you shop?" She'd told him that they did, but these smelled and tasted so much better. "Sure they do. And full of bugs and spiders no doubt, too. Don't feed me any of that crap when we move in together. I'll not let you cook for me if you do."

Annabelle could still see the look on Emerald's face when he said that. She'd been shocked at first, then furious. When she walked to the door and opened it, the man laughed.

"Get out." He laughed harder. "I'm dead serious. I want you out of here. And, as I have said to you over and over, never call me again. What makes you think that I'd let you move into my apartment, much less cook for you? I have a full time job that I love, and I don't have time to cater to some two hundred-thousand year old Neanderthal who thinks the little woman should be barefoot and pregnant to simply wait on him. And—this is the real kicker—I did not invite you here at all, much less to insult us."

When the young man laughed again, Emerald growled. He stood up, but Annabelle didn't think the man was taking Emerald seriously. He tried to put his arms around her but she shoved him back. Annabelle had wanted to intervene on the man's part, as she could see Emerald's wolf running along her skin, but Emerald shook her head.

"Now, let's not fight. Come on. You know I'd never expect you to cook for me. And the garden? If it makes you happy, I'm okay with it too. Just don't serve me up any." He reached for her again, and then Annabelle could see that he was getting mad. "This is not the time or the place to have this conversation. Let's just have a nice time here, and we'll talk—"

"I am not going to tell you again to get out of here. And you're not to call me or contact me in any way. I know for a fact that you were told several times by the police to back the fuck off." He took a step toward Emerald, and she flinched from him. In that moment Annabelle knew that he'd hit her before. "Get out."

Annabelle had no idea what the young man—his name was Nolan, she just remembered—would have done to either of them had Allen not stepped through the open door. He looked at Emerald, then at the young man, before standing in front of her granddaughter.

"I think you've overstayed your welcome, young man, and now would be a good time to get out. As you've been asked to do several times now." Nolan looked like he might have said more, but Blair and Josh both came into the kitchen from the dining room. "You heard me. It's time you left. And it might be best if you never returned."

He looked pissed when he looked at her. Annabelle nearly took a step back, but he looked at Emerald then. If looks could cause harm, she'd have been seriously injured. She had wondered then and now how badly the man had hurt her granddaughter.

"You're making the biggest mistake of your life, Emerald. You know it and I know it. Call off the family and I'll forget this whole thing." She lifted her chin and he laughed. "We'll see how this ends for us. I told you that we're going to be together, and now we have unfinished business, you and I. Just remember that you've been warned."

After he left the house, peeling out of the driveway and spraying rocks everywhere, Emerald had looked at all of them. Annabelle's heart broke for her granddaughter and still hurt for her. She left them then, just went to her car and left. As far as Annabelle knew, she'd not been back since.

Celeste coming down the hall made her stand up. Annabelle reached for Emerald again, but she told her she was too upset to talk now. Celeste was smiling hugely when she pulled her into her arms for a hug.

"He's going to come with us. I'll have to set him up in a hotel, but he's coming with us. I'm so…do you think your family will mind that he's there too?" Before she could tell her they'd love it, Celeste was talking again. "I just couldn't believe it. He said that he missed spending time with me, and thought that since I was going to France in a couple of weeks he'd spend some time with me if I didn't mind. If I didn't mind? My goodness, I wanted to scream at him how much I didn't mind. What do you think of that?"

"I think the family would welcome him in the house. And there is no reason for him to be put in a hotel. One of my granddaughters is a doctor and another one is a nurse. He'll get the best of care." Celeste nodded and was so happy that Annabelle couldn't help but be happy for her too. "He'll love it there so much, he might want to move in with them."

"Oh, that would be lovely, just lovely." As they made arrangements with his doctor to have him released, Annabelle let Sapphire and Blair know what was going on. They were, of course, thrilled and would welcome them both with open arms. The only concern they had was if he knew about them.

"Not that I'm aware of. So far as I know, Celeste doesn't either." Sapphire laughed when she told them that she thought it was time to tell her old friend. "What could happen other than she'd have a massive heart attack and have to be converted?"

~~~

Emerald moved up her stairs, thinking about how much longer she was going to live there. There was so much she'd accumulated over the year and a half she'd lived here, and she was going to hate packing it up…especially as sore as she was. Going up the last step, she looked around the corner to make sure that Nolan wasn't lurking in the corners again. The last time had been bad enough.

Entering her apartment, she closed the door behind her and leaned heavily against it. She needed to shift, but more than that, she wanted to shift and run. But there was no place for her to do that here in the city, and less now that her entire family was watching her.

She supposed she could have gone home today and healed herself, but she'd been leery of going home now with Allen there watching her. He'd been keeping an especially close eye on her since that day at the house, going so far as to come to the school because of "just being in the neighborhood" and wanting to talk to her. He never had anything more to say to her than the garden was doing well.

And Nolan wasn't backing off, no matter what she did to keep him away. When she'd left this morning, being trapped by Nolan in the hall, it had taken everything she had to get away. Now she was hurting badly for not paying attention to her surroundings. She was careful now, however.

Stripping down to her skin as soon as she moved into her apartment, she let her wolf take her as she moaned through the pain. Not the shift, never that, but the pain of the beating she'd taken that morning. And it had been one hell of a beating.

Wandering around her two rooms, she stretched and let her wolf have her way. It was cramped, yes, but she was feeling better all the time. When she hopped up on her bed and laid out, she wanted to close her eyes and sleep for a month, but there were papers to grade as well as a few loads of laundry to do. But the longer she lay there, the less important those things became.

*You've been a fool, you know that right?* Her wolf only hummed her agreement to her. *Why is it that I pick the worst guys? And the ones with the biggest fists? Or worst yet, why is it that guys that are horrible just seem to latch right onto me? Tell me that? I'm not a bad person, so why do I attract the bad elements all the time?*

Still no answer, but Emerald knew that it was her fault. Not the beatings. She never dated a man more than once if he hit her. But she'd never dated Nolan Bruce…he just had never taken her no to heart. He just would not give up on trying to see her.

*I blame it on my family.* She giggled at that. *Not him coming around, but the need to have some sort of love in my life. I just wanted to have a nice night out, and he came barging into my life. But he's not listening to me no matter how many times I tell him I do not want him near me.*

He wasn't either. Every day since she'd kicked him out of her family's house, he'd been emailing or calling her, even texting…and she had no idea how he'd gotten her information. She'd not even invited him to the house that day, but he'd shown up on his own and came in as if he owned the place. It had started even before that, when she'd been out with a friend and he'd decided that she was the one. One what, she'd never been able to figure out. He wasn't her mate.

Today wasn't the first time she'd actually seen him since then. Nor was it the first, second, or even third time he'd hit her. She'd been taking beatings from him for about a month now. Anytime she wasn't paying attention, he'd pop out of nowhere and beat the shit out of her because she wouldn't sleep with him. Fucking bastard was going to get himself killed if she ever was in a place she could let her wolf tear his ass up.

*What is it with men and sex?* Her wolf growled low. *I mean seriously, is it that good?* She'd never know, she thought to herself, because even if the right man did come along that she wanted to get laid by, Nolan would hurt them. He had before.

*That poor man.* She'd only met the nice man at the bar to get a drink with him. Shaffer Carlee had met her at the bar in Tenth, a block from her house, when Nolan had confronted them both. The bar wasn't a place that she went to often, but Shaffer was well known there because he delivered their orders weekly. Nolan had been tossed out almost as soon as he started screaming at her that they were married; which, of course, they were not. Things had gotten ugly fast when he punched her in the mouth for "back talking" him, as he'd told her.

Then Nolan had nearly beaten Shaffer to death when they'd left the bar. He'd told Shaffer to stay away from her, but Shaffer had told him that he needed help and to stay away from them both. The fight was bad and only got worse as Nolan brought out a bat and began beating Shaffer, then her with it. She might have killed him herself had it not been for the crowd of people that had come out to watch them get the shit beaten out of them.

*I'm a first-class loser.* Her wolf stretched out, and Emerald pulled her into her, shifting back to herself in a matter of seconds. She lay on her bed naked, wondering what the hell was wrong with her. "I can't date anyone for fear of Nolan, and I don't dare tell my family, even though I'm pretty sure they are aware now that he's hit me and that I'm afraid for my life. It would be funny if it wasn't so fucking scary. What am I supposed to do now?"

Of course her wolf had no answer. Closing her eyes, she thought of all the crap she had to do and how much she had no desire to get up and do it. But she had to. There were no grandma's living here to help her out.

Emerald got up and pulled out something soft and comfortable to put on. Then she went to get her laundry basket. Maybe if she washed enough to get her to the weekend she could finish it up when she had more time. Instead of listening to her reasoning, she knew that she'd end up doing it all tonight and grade all the papers too. Life on your own, she thought, sure was busy.

"I suck." She grinned to herself as she pulled out the phone. "At least I can have pizza anyway I want it, and no one cares if I have onion breath."

Emerald was pulling on her sweats as she ordered her extra-large triple meat pizza. And for dessert she remembered her grandmother had sent her some of her lemon cookies in a big tin. She got that down now and started munching on them. She was smiling to herself when she realized her grandmother would have a fit if she could see her now.

"No eating sweets before dinner." She laughed at her voice as she imitated her grandmother. "And you'll tie your hair up so that that pizza man doesn't think you're a homeless person."

She had pointed out that homeless people didn't have pizzas delivered to their homes with an address, and she huffed at her. Grandmother was making a point then and it still made her laugh.

The pizza came about ten minutes later than she had expected it. She was afraid that Nolan had waylaid her dinner, but the elevator wasn't working again and the guy had had to climb the five flights of stairs to get it to her. Emerald gave him an extra ten bucks for his trouble, and had to nearly close the door in his face to get him to leave. He was nearly drooling on her pie.

"You'd think he'd get sick of pizza working there." Emerald sat down with her beer and took her first bite. "Man this is good. No wonder he wanted to stay and help me eat it."

Emerald was talking to herself again. She'd not done it in a very long time, not since her parents had both been killed. But lately she'd been having entire conversations with herself, going as far as to answer her questions too. There was no reason for it. If she needed someone to talk to, she could have simply reached for some family member, but that wasn't as easy lately as it once had been.

"They have their own families and stuff going on in their lives." Emerald looked down at her nearly finished dinner. "They don't need a fifth wheel mucking things up for them. Besides, I'm pretty sure they're glad I'm not bothering them all the time. Sheesh, I'm boring."

Laughing, she finished off the last piece and put the empty box in the trash. She was hesitant about taking it out as it was dark now, but she did gather it up to take out in the morning. As she was setting the last of the other trash near her door to take out, someone knocked on her door hard enough to make the hinges shake.

"Let me in, Emerald. I want to talk to you." Nolan shouted at her twice more before she heard someone tell him to go away. "I'm not talking to you. Butt the fuck out."

Mrs. Grosshandler, the woman who lived right across from her, shouted at him to go away again, and Emerald almost opened the door to make sure she was safe when her son spoke. He told Nolan to get the hell out of there before he called the police.

"This is all her fault. Tell her to open the fucking door and I'll go in and talk to her." She was standing next to the door when he pounded his fist against it again. "Open the door, Emerald, or so help me, I'll make you pay."

She wanted to cry. Emerald wanted to tell him to leave her alone, but that would only keep him there longer. Or worse, have him busting down the door again to get to her. She just wanted him to leave her alone. This was simply getting out of hand. What the hell had she done to make him do this to her?

When it finally got quiet on the other side of her door, she moved to her couch and sat down. It was too late for her to grade papers, and she was too depressed to watch television. Instead, she sat there in the dark, wondering why her life was so screwed up...why she couldn't meet the man of her dreams like her sisters had.

"Because you're a loser. I think we've had this conversation before." Her wolf growled at her. "Oh, be quiet. You know as well as I do that the only type of men we attract are the kind that hit first and asks questions, if they have any, later. We're gonna spend our whole lives wondering why we're alone, too."

Closing her eyes, she laid down. She really was depressed. Emerald even thought about calling off work tomorrow, but knew that she wouldn't. Not that she needed the money, because she wasn't getting paid all that much and what little there was went right back into the class. The volunteers were helping out now. Not just with her class, but all three of the summer classes that were being held. And she was glad for that. But in five weeks the summer was over, and she'd be going back to the pack school. She was already looking forward to it.

Letting sleep take her, she thought of her family again before sliding away. Emerald decided that she was going to be the favorite aunt. All her sisters' children would come to her and she'd love it. Yeah, she thought, I'm going to have a family even if I have to pretend they're mine.

# Chapter 3

The house was huge. No, that wasn't right, it was monstrous. And it wasn't a house so much as it was a home. This was just what he'd been looking for when he'd been house hunting a few months ago.

"It's a bit overwhelming, I know." He smiled at Blair, who had picked him and his mom up at the airport along with Annabelle. "Sapphire and her family had purchased it before I met her. And I'm glad. It's perfect for us."

"It certainly can hold you all." Blair nodded and got out of the limo on his side. Jul was impressed with the big man. He wore his wealth like a skin. It fit him well and he wasn't uncomfortable with it. "You've lived here since you two got married, then?"

Blair helped him with his luggage and said he had. "As I said, Sapphire lived here first, and when we met, I moved in with them. The house needed some major help, and we've had a good time fixing it up."

It looked it too. Well-loved came to mind as he made his way up the front steps. And upon entering the stately home, he was shocked to see that the inside matched the outside in size and how it was well cared for. He ran his hand over the curved oak stair rail. Jul looked up the double staircase and wondered if any of them slid down it just for fun, and frowned. He had no idea where that might have come from.

"We've put you on the second floor. The room is finished with its remodel, and since Emerald isn't living here any longer we thought you'd like the room." They entered the room and Jul smiled as Blair continued. "She really liked earth tones, and we were trying to lure her back with them."

"It's beautiful." Blair nodded and put his luggage on the bed. "Why doesn't she live here? Married?"

"No. She's the baby of the girls, and wants to...you know? I'm not really sure. Something about us needing our own space. I wonder if she remembers how many people are in and out of here every day." Blair grinned. "She's supposed to come down tomorrow for dinner. She won't stay, but we are looking forward to seeing her. School and all."

Jul nodded. He remembered going to school and wanting to be independent. He'd had a good deal more fun than he should have, and wondered if this Emerald was as well. Jul thought about having a word or two with her about studying hard, but nixed that idea. He was a visitor, not family.

After Blair left, Jul put his things away. He didn't live out of a suitcase well, and wasn't going to do it here. This place screamed comfort and homey, and he was going to enjoy it. Pulling out his computer, he put it on the large desk. The room also had an Internet hook up, Blair had told him, and he had to work hard at not hurting himself while he plugged into it.

The gunshot wound wasn't bad...not as bad as it could have been, he supposed. But it still hurt. He'd taken a bullet to his ribs, and while it had been a through and through, he'd still gotten two broken ribs from it. Sitting down while things booted up, he looked around the room again.

The spread was a dark brown with gold flecks in it. The shams at the top were gold, with dark brown flecks. The rugs on the hardwood floors were browns and reds, with blue in them as well. The chairs at the fireplace were the same hue of blue as the rug, and all the curtains were dark green and blue to bring it all together. The walls were the most beautiful shade of sunset red he'd ever seen. When his computer signaled it was ready, he opened his email, tearing his eyes away from the soothing tones of the room.

There were three from Colby and one from his lawyer. He opened that one first. Jul smiled as he read his congratulations from him.

"I will buy the person who talked you into going at this alone a case of their favorite champagne as soon as you tell me you're really going to do this. I'm assuming that you know that things will go very well for you, and you'll have a great deal of fun getting things going. Your father would be so proud of you. Well done, my boy."

He went on to tell him all he'd have to do, and what was needed from him to get the ball rolling. It wasn't as simple as him taking off Dan's name over the door...which, he supposed, he had to do anyway. But he would have to do something with the label as well. Dan had decided, after a long talk with his family, to lend the name to his son-in-law to see about getting his own wines going. But as Dan had said, it would be a short trial; the son wasn't any good at anything. It was no longer going to be called Whitney and Williams Wines, so now Jul would have to come up with something different. And of course, pay the name change fee.

A knock at the door interrupted him while reading the last email from Colby, telling him that the grapes in France were doing well. And he too talked about what the new label would be. There were five for him to look at that their art department had come up with, none of which Jul cared all that much for. He decided to see if he could find a firm to help him with that, as his department consisted of a single man about seventy years old that thought change was bad for your indigestion. Whatever that meant. Jul was told by the lovely young woman—he thought her name was Jade—that dinner was ready.

Dinner was a big affair at the Henson household, apparently. His mom was there, of course, as was most of the rest of the family. They had said that Emerald should be there, but she was behind in her papers and would be out tomorrow. Saturday, apparently, was her only day off. Jul sat at the end of the table between two men he'd just met, Quentin and Thad, who introduced him to their wives.

By the time the first platter was brought in, Jul felt as if he'd known these men his entire life. Both were successful businessmen, and were very helpful in answering a couple of questions he'd had about going into business on his own. Deciding that they were pretty savvy about such matters, he asked Thad about an advertising firm.

"You're having dinner with two of the largest. Have you heard of Flair Marketing?" He nodded. "That is the sole owner. And Marketing Gems? That would be his wife. The two of them have made millions off bringing a business out of the toilet and making the owners a hefty profit as well. Those two can make a business more money with just a month of work than anyone I've ever used."

"You use them?" Thad smiled and nodded. "And their fees? Are they reasonable, or now that they're huge do they charge more?"

"I guarantee you, if you use them, no matter the price, you'll sing their praises. And no, they are extremely inexpensive. And Josh over there, Ruby's husband, said that if they just give him the go ahead, he'll double, maybe even triple, their profit margins. But they want to stay like they are. Hometown friendly with enough money so as not to ever have to worry about it."

Jul liked that. He even liked the people he would more than likely be working with. They really were down home and extremely friendly. And not a one of them treated him or his mom like they were anything but their family. It was a wonderful feeling, one he was afraid he could get used to very easily.

As they moved from dinner to dessert, he decided that if he stayed here long, he'd weigh a ton and have to resist the temptation of a second piece of cherry pie that was still warm with ice cream melting over it. He groaned when someone suggested they move to the deck surrounding the house. He was nearly too full to move.

"You mending all right there, boy?" He grinned at Allen, the patriarch of the family but not the sole master of the house. Jul had already figured out that Mrs. Erickson ran this place. "Heard you tangled with the wrong sort of element up there in that big city."

"I did. He jumped me on my way out of my work. I did manage to take him down, despite him putting a bullet in me." He lifted his shirt up when Allen asked to see it. "It's the ribs that hurt the most. The wound isn't so bad."

"You need to be in a safer environment. People around here would never pull a gun on you. They might jump you and tear into you a little, but they would only be playing." Jul wondered what he meant by that but nodded. "You have a nice mom. She worries about you too. You shouldn't make your mom worry about you."

"I try not to, but there are bad people everywhere." He looked around. "I bet you guys don't have a lot of trouble with people trying to rob you. The men in this family are fairly big, aren't they?"

"It's the breed. Blair comes from good stock and his animal is master. It's good, too, for as many people as he has under him." Jul nodded. The man was very strange, and he wondered if anyone else had any trouble talking to him when he continued. "Thad tells me you're in the wine business."

"Yes. I have my own label. And we also have a line of crackers and cheese. I was going to talk to Blair and Sapphire about coming up with a new logo and label. My partner…well, my father's partner…retired a few months back, and I'm going to keep the business going on my own."

"They'd be good at it. My little Sapphire can take a trash heap and make it shine. Never seen a woman that could come up with more ideas that would make you money. And Blair, he's got a head on his shoulders about how to put that stuff out there that will make you wonder if he's not magical. That would be Opal, by the way." Again Jul was confused as he glanced at the woman. Her belly was round with her and Sloan's first child, and the man was so besotted with his wife that it was a treat to watch them together. In fact, all of them seemed to be deeply in love with each other.

As the night wore on, so did his exhaustion. Jul stood up when the rest of them did and said he was going to bed. He hurt a little more than he wanted to admit, and as soon as he got to his room, he took the pain pills that he'd been given at the hospital and laid down. He was asleep almost as soon as his head hit the pillow.

~~~

Nolan was going to find her if it was the last thing he did. No one was going to turn him out, and that was final. And this bitch had it coming.

As soon as she came out of her work, Nolan stepped in front of her. Before she could scream, he put the gun to her forehead.

"Hello there, sweetie." Tears streamed down her face and he wanted to lick them off her. But that would put him a little closer than he wanted to be to her. To be honest, he couldn't remember her name, but she was the most recent one of the bitches that had left him high and dry. "You and I are going to finish what we started."

"No, please don't do this. I don't want you to hurt me again. I called the police because you gave me no choice."

He laughed at that. But he did want to hurt her, and that was the fucking point.

Running the barrel down her face to her mouth, he made her take it. Fucking her with the gun had him as hard as rock, but he needed more before this was finished. Pulling her body to his, he squeezed her breast until she cried out. Then he twisted it hard enough to have her scream. Yes, this was what he wanted. For her to be in so much pain that she cried out for it. As he pulled her shirt up so he could bite her too, a noise behind him made him turn, using her as a shield.

"What the fuck are you doing?" He tried to hide behind the woman, but she was too fucking short, and it was all he could do to hold her still. The man took several steps toward them until Nolan pointed the gun at him. "Let her go and there won't be any problems."

"There aren't any now so far as I can see." The man moved toward him again and Nolan put the gun to her head. "She and I have some unfinished business, and if you want to live, then I would suggest that you go away and forget that you ever saw us."

"I can't do that." Nolan told him to go away again. "I can't. She won't live if I leave here, and I won't be able to live with myself knowing that I could have done something to save her."

"Your loss." He fired the gun to her head and dropped the woman before he shot at the man. He knew that he'd not killed him right away, and walked toward him just as the man pulled his own gun. Nolan stared at him for too long and felt the bite of the bullet before he fired at the man again. Christ, where in the hell had that come from? No one shot him, damn it. After firing for a third time at the ground, he took off. Christ, he'd actually shot him. The motherfucker shot him.

As he limped away, his body burning from the pain, he tried to think what the fuck he was going to do now. He was fucking bleeding all over the place, he hurt like hell, and he'd not had his fun. But that had to be secondary to the fact that the motherfucker had actually shot him. Nolan made his way to his apartment and locked the door behind him before he got a chance to look at the wound.

"Motherfucking cock sucker." The blood staining the front of his shirt scared him a lot, so he stripped down and went to the kitchen. The bullet had torn into his side and left a long streak of open meat. Running his finger under his bloodied wound, he licked the blood off his finger and hummed out his approval. If he couldn't have fun with the bitch, then having his fun this way would have to do.

He pulled off his pants and wrapped his bloody hand around his cock. He was painfully hard, yet so excited that he could hardly contain himself. Closing his eyes, he wished that he'd looked back at the bitch at least once so he'd have the image in his mind, but the man would have to do. There he saw what he needed.

The first bullet had hit the man in the chest. He could see the stain on his shirt as if he were there with him. As he thought about how the man was dying, his blood pooling under his body, Nolan fisted his cock harder and faster. As soon as he grabbed his open wound at his side with his free hand, Nolan cried out with the pain and the release. His cum shot out of his dick so hard that he had to hang onto the sink for several moments after.

Sitting down on the only chair, he leaned his head against the table. It had been an amazing rush, but it was short lived. He'd wanted to play and the man had interrupted it. As he sat there, he heard the sirens screaming down the street and knew that they were going to be extremely disappointed that they'd wasted the gas to get there. Both of them were dead. He'd bet his next climax on it.

Standing up, he staggered to the refrigerator and pulled out a bottle of water. Draining it, he reached for a second one and drank from it as he made his way to the living room. He pulled on his underwear as he walked. Sitting on the couch, he thought about the bitch and pulled his notebook out from between the cushions.

Nolan prided himself on being a different kind of murderer. He knew what he was and embraced the sanity of it. He wasn't crazy by any stretch of the imagination, but he was having a good time. Flipping through the pictures, he found the bitch that he'd shot.

"Margo Winter." He put a mark over her picture and then wrote how he had shot her in the head. He also gave her only one star. She couldn't have four stars as he usually gave one of his murders because she'd not gotten him off…the man had. Stuffing it back between the cushions, he leaned back.

He supposed he should have gotten his wound cleaned up, but he was too exhausted after that amazing climax. Smiling to himself, he heard another siren going by his place and wondered if they would do a door to door search. That made him sit up. He'd have to clean up if he was going to have his moment. Going to his bedroom, he pulled out his first aid kit and began working on cleaning himself up.

It took him nearly twenty minutes to get it cleaned up, and another ten to find a bandage that would fit over it. By the time he was finished, he was sweating and sick to his stomach. Instead of going back to the couch, he went to his kitchen and pulled out the array of painkillers he'd gotten over his span as a killer.

His job as a cable installer had allowed him entrance into the best places to steal things. Mostly he only took small things—drugs for instance. Then there was the occasional wad of cash. To his way of thinking, if you left it out, then it was his. And being that he loved this part of his job, he was always very careful of what he took and what he might leave behind when he did.

He pulled out some oxycodone and took two of them. He knew it was a lot, but he was hurting now and figured a nice nap would do him so much good. Going back to the living room, he put a pillow over the small stain of blood and then lay down again. But before sleep could claim him, he picked up his notebook and placed it under the floorboards where it was always stored. No one would ever find it there.

He had no idea how long he slept, but it was dark out and he was sore when he woke. Getting up, he went to the bathroom and noticed that his bandage was soaked through, so he peeled it off and replaced it. He was still buzzing from the drugs earlier and didn't take more now, tempting though it might be. He was in the living room again, dressed now, when someone knocked on his door.

Peeking through the eye hole, he grinned. It was time to be the helpful neighbor again. In his neighborhood, this was more common than not having the police coming to your door. He pulled the chain off and looked around once before opening. Tossing his coat to the couch, he covered the new stain and smiled as he widened the opening of the door.

"Officer?" The cop nodded once as he looked over Nolan's shoulder. "Can I help you? It's kind of late for you guys to be collecting for the policemen's thing, don't you think?"

"We're going around talking to all your neighbors to see if you've heard anything in the last couple of hours." Nolan wondered how long it had actually been but shook his head. "Nothing out of the ordinary?"

"I just woke up. I've been fighting a cold off and on for the past few days, and have been taking some night time stuff. Knocks me right out." The officer looked over his shoulder again. "Would you like to come in? I assure you that I'm not harboring any kind of bad element."

"No. We have a good description of the guy. Won't be long before we apprehend him. People like that don't last long on the streets." Nolan nodded, but his mind was racing. "We have an artist on the job right now, and will have something to bring around later. I'm assuming you're going to be around?"

Nolan nodded. "I don't know how much help I can be. I've been here, as I've said." He knew that his smile was tight, he could feel it, but he wasn't sure what to make of this new development.

After the cop left, telling him that he'd be back in a bit, Nolan sat down on the edge of his couch and tried to think. A description? Was it possible that the woman wasn't dead? No, he was sure the bullet had gone into her skull, and at the temple as well. The man he'd shot in the chest, twice for sure, but he had to think where it had been. Where the fuck was the heart anyway?

Standing up, he pretended to do the pledge he'd done in school a long time ago, and had trouble even remembering what hand he'd put where. Finally, he put his finger over his pulse at his throat and wondered if it was faster the closer it got to the heart. But he was at a loss. Mother fuck, maybe he'd shot him in the wrong side of his body. Was it even possible at that range that the fucker was still alive?

"Nobody was alive when I left." He was sure of it. But the more he thought of it, the less sure he was becoming. Pacing around, he decided to go down to the scene and see what was going on. Surely someone there would know something.

It took him fifteen minutes to make his way through the crowd. Nolan had to make himself not tell anyone this was his handiwork, but it was difficult when everyone he passed was running their mouth about who it might have been. There were six cruisers there, and even two ambulances. Christ, he might just get off from that alone. But as he made his way to the front of the line, he could hear what the others were saying, and none of it was terribly helpful.

"She was shot in the head but could live." "They said the man shot her because it was a lover's quarrel or something." He looked at the person talking and wondered how the hell they had come to that. But the rumors were more violent the closer he got to the tape. "He was raping her when this other guy came up and wanted to join them. Shot them both." "A spray of a machine gun nearly took their heads off. Hard to believe they're still alive." That was the dumbest thing he'd heard so far.

The officer that was manning the yellow tape was watching the crowd but said little. Mostly he told the crowd to stand back, or even to go on home, there was little to see. A woman asked him if they were both dead and he shook his head. That didn't help Nolan at all. Both of them had seen him, and even if one of them talked, he was so fucked up. Finally the sea of blue uniforms parted and he could see the stain on the alley. There wasn't as much as he'd hoped from the man and the woman...he saw nothing as someone closed the gap almost as quickly as it had parted.

"She was shot in the shoulder." He looked at the man standing next to him. "The woman, somebody shot her in the shoulder. The man was shot in the chest, but they said it was nothing major, that he'd be all right in a few days. They were damned lucky, they were. Someone called the cops almost as soon as the guy was running his fucking ass away from them."

"How did you find out? I thought they were not saying much." The man showed him a small device a little larger than a cell phone. "What is that?"

"It's a scanner. Got it real cheap a few days ago, and can hear them talking to each other." He let him hear the next message that came through. It was about a robbery on Englewood Avenue. "I can avoid the cops by knowing just about where they're gonna be. And if I need me a little excitement — too much of that nowadays, if you ask me — I just mosey on down to a crime scene and have me a look see."

Nolan wanted one. Not just to hear where they were going to be, but what transpired after he finished with his fun. Christ, he was hard just thinking about it. As the man held it to his ear, Nolan made his way out of the crowd and to the electronics store a few blocks from where he lived. He figured he'd pay just about any price just to have himself a way to get off more than once.

It cost him forty-one dollars and ten cents. Of course he'd needed the head phones that were a must, as well as the charger. He was nearly out the door with his new toys when he looked over at one of the television sets they had running. He watched it as the bitch he'd shot was talking to a news anchor.

"He just shot me. I didn't even know who he was, not until he said that we were going to finish something we'd started." The anchor woman asked her what that might be. "I have no idea. He looks like some jerk I met in a bar once, but that never went anywhere. And that poor man who tried to help. Is he going to be all right?"

Nolan was bumped from behind and moved so the old biddy could get out of the store. By the time he looked at the set again, they were running a thing for tampons or some shit he didn't care about. Nolan had no idea if the woman had answered his bitch or not.

"She has to be taken care of." He moved out of the store when the clerk looked at him oddly. He also had to make arrangements to see about the man. It was stupid of him to have left without checking them, he knew that now, but what was done was done. Now he had to clean up his mess. Nolan was going to finish the business with the woman if it was all he got done.

Going back to his apartment, he pulled out his notebook and went to the page where the bitch was. He'd have to either mess up his system or complete the job as soon as possible. He opted for completing the job. Turning on his new scanner, he smiled when he heard about the robbery turned shooting on Englewood. This was much better than having a television with porn on it all the time.

Yes, he thought, this was going to be so much fun. As the radio blasted out another issue, he sat down and freed his cock. He was jerking off to a carjacking, and laughed at the way it sounded when said aloud. Nolan was in heaven. And now that he had his little toys, he was going to be in heaven every chance he got.

# Chapter 4

Emerald had an hour to go before she was finished for the weekend. Her body was tired and she wanted to take a nap so desperately that she'd nearly fallen asleep in the teachers' lounge earlier. But as soon as she left here, there was the trip to her sister's, something she was looking forward to and dreading at the same time. She loved her family...very much so, but they were just too much for her right now. Not that she didn't enjoy playing with little Carter. He was a hoot, but the rest of them were forever asking her about her life. Her personal life.

When one of the students raised their hand, Emerald nodded to him just as her sister Jade touched her mind.

*Thought you'd like to know that we have a couple of people staying with us. A guy who has been shot and his mom. She's wonderful. He's this guy who looks like he is slightly overwhelmed by all of us.* Emerald laughed with her sister as her student asked to go to the bathroom. *You're still coming over tonight, right? I have big plans for us.*

*I'm leaving here and coming straight there. I have about three loads of laundry to finish up, but I'm sure that Sapphire won't mind if I do them there.* Jade just laughed. *I'm trying to be independent. It's hard, you know. And the laundry place where I'm living is out of order again.*

It wasn't, but she was a little afraid to go down there alone. Nolan had been standing outside her apartment building this morning, and when she'd taken the kids out on the playground after lunch, she was sure he'd been lurking about then too. The man was going to get himself killed if he didn't fucking leave her alone.

*I guess. I can't wait until you find your own mate and can be as happy as the rest of us are.* Emerald felt the pain her heart. She wanted to ask her sister what made her think she wasn't happy now, but didn't. *Also, I'm supposed to remind you that we have that ball thing next weekend, and Sapphire and Grandmother are counting on you to be there. Dressed to kill, they said.*

She'd forgotten about that. It was a charity thing her grandmother had started last year to raise money for the children in the pack, as well as some of the townspeople too. Some of the kids had only a single parent, and a few of them were living with their grandparents. Most of them had come from a pack that Blair had taken over a few years ago.

*I'll be there this weekend. Do you think you can loan me a dress for this ball? I have that blue one, but Sapphire said if I wear it to a function again, she'll buy me something and I won't like it.* Jade told her she thought she had one she could use. *Oh, and so you know, there is some buzz going around about the two empty buildings downtown. Did you or anyone there put a bid on them? The one that was the old school might be good for an office building. Tell Blair if he buys them, I want to rent one from him.*

*For what?* Before she could tell her sister it was none of her business, Jade cut herself off. *I have to go. There's a bear in the woods.*

It wasn't a metaphor for her sister. Jade worked for the parks department for the state, and literally chased bears and other creatures off when necessary. Mostly she worked at home or with Quentin, but she did help out the parks department when they really needed her to. Her husband, Quentin, didn't care for it much, but he knew she could handle herself.

After closing the connection to her sister, she started working on the papers that had been turned in. Her volunteer had not shown up today either, but her mind kept drifting to the building. She wanted to see if she could change it into small shops, like a consignment place for some of the locals. It was a silly idea but Emerald thought it would be a way for her to make some money as well as for some of the people around town to save some.

"Ms. E, do you think it would be okay if I stayed here tonight?" She looked at the little boy, Connor Shoot, and noticed, not for the first time, the bruises on his throat and arms. "I like it here. It's real quiet, and there is that big rug over there I can sleep on."

"I know you do, honey, but there are rules. Where is your daddy this week? Is he home again?" Connor nodded and looked around the room as if he expected him to be right there. Her heart broke a little for him. "I'm really sorry, Connor, but you know that you can't do that. What if there was a fire or something? How would you get out?"

He didn't answer her, but she could see the sadness in his eyes, and the terror. There was very little she could do to help him other than to report it to the school nurse. Very little legally anyway. But she could try and do something with the help of her family.

All the kids in her room were from, for the most part, harsh homes. Even little Shayla, whose father had put up the big stink during parent/teacher conferences, had a rough life. Her dad was working now, but for most of the year he was home, and his temper wasn't all that good even under the best of circumstances. Emerald had no idea if he hit the child. She'd never seen any marks on her, but he did knock the wife around. Not that it was any better, but she hated abuse of any kind to children.

"Let me see what I can do for you." She opened her top drawer and pulled out the bag of candy bars that she'd brought in that morning. "Why don't you do me a favor and pass these around? My sister gave them to me, and she knows that I'm dieting."

Grinning, he took them to the other students. It was a lie. She could eat several bags of candy a day and not gain an ounce. Her metabolism was very high, and her being a wolf helped too. She knew that most of these kids only got the meal provided to them by the state, and rarely had a treat such as a candy bar. As they munched quietly on their treat, she reached for Sloan.

*I have a situation that I need you to help me with.* He laughed and asked her if she knew it was the middle of the afternoon. *Sure, but this way I know you're alone and not in bed with my sister.*

*Ah. So you think?* She felt herself flush when he laughed. *You know that I would do most anything for my favorite sister-*

*in-law. You need only to give me a list of who you want murdered and I'll see to it.*

Emerald thought of the one person she would love to have murdered. Well, maybe not murdered, but hurt badly. Nolan was going to have to be dealt with, and soon. It was becoming a real problem for her, and she was getting sick of leaving by the bathroom door. It was the only way she'd made it to work on time. Things had to get better or she was—

*Emerald? What is it? I can feel your anxiety.* She let out a long breath before answering him, but he was worried now and she could tell. *Emerald?*

*I'm fine. I swear it, but I have a student that I'm concerned for. The poor little boy is being abused. He's afraid to go home, and wants to stay here over the weekend. I can't do that, as you know, but I hate that he's that afraid that he'd stay in a locked building rather than go home.* He told her most kids hated to be home and asked her how this one was different. *His dad beats the shit out of him, and I'm pretty sure that his sister might be in the same boat.*

That got his attention apparently. *Who is his father, and where might I find him? You know how much I hate the abuse of little ones. And with my own child on the way, it's been harder and harder for me to turn my back on them.*

*I know that. And I wouldn't ask, but the little boy has a mark around his neck that smells like hemp. I think he's tying the little guy up. Why would anyone do that to such a little person? Have they no compassion?* She felt his explosive anger and almost regretted telling him. *I don't want you to kill him, Sloan. Just show him the errors of his ways.*

*Oh, I plan to do that.* She told him the address and the little boy's name when he asked her again. *This child, does he have all he needs? You think that he will need some items to get him through the rest of the summer? I will make sure before I leave them that he is well taken care of. His sister too, if need be.*

*I honestly don't know. I get him the school supplies he needs. Most of the kids in this school have very little to get by on, but I supply what I can. Lunches are free for most of them, but it doesn't fill the void for the entire day.* She felt the tears and had to pick up a book to hide them from the children. *I want to take them all home with me and care for them. I know I can't, but I want to. Why do people do this to their own children?*

*I'm sorry, honey, but I know you do. And I hurt for you as well as the little children. Does Blair or the rest of them know that you're paying for things that should be supplied?* She told him no, but it was none of their business anyway. *You know that it is. If you need help with this, we'd be more than glad to help out. You shouldn't be doing this alone. I could make sure your class has everything they need, and it won't be a hardship on us at all.*

*It's no hardship on me at all. I love what I do, Sloan. I just wish I could do more.* He said he understood and would take care of this for her.

When she closed the connection, she went to the ladies' room and splashed water on her face. As she made her way back to her room, she saw someone lurking outside on the playground. It was Nolan.

As she moved back against the wall, she tried to think what to do. Going to the classroom was out because if he got in, she didn't want the children to be hurt. Just as she was going to shift and go out and kick his ass, another teacher came around the corner and startled her.

"There's a man out there." She pointed to Nolan as he moved to another door to try and open it by jerking on it as hard as he could. "Are all the doors secure?"

"I'll be calling the police even if they are." He pulled out his cell and made the call. "You go on and get to your room. Tell those other two teachers to lock down. The intercom here don't work so good no more."

Emerald nodded and went to the first room. The teacher was in the middle of reading a book to her class, and Emerald walked up to her to give her the news. She was less than gracious.

"I guess this means we'll have to wait around for the police, then fill out paperwork again. This really fucks up my day. Christ, this school sucks. If I could find another one that would take me, I'd be there in a second." She told the kids to get into their positions, then looked at her again. "I suppose you want me to show you what to do? Or are you expecting me to do it for you? You get them kids hurt and it'll be your ass that'll be paying up, not mine. Go away."

Emerald didn't bother saying anything to her, but left. She got a much better welcome for the news from the next teacher. As she was leaving, however, she asked her if she thought the police would come into her room.

"Why?" The woman looked around, then went to her desk. Emerald looked as well and couldn't believe what she saw there. "Is that marijuana? Are you actually smoking that on school grounds?"

The teacher shrugged as if it shouldn't matter to anyone. "There are days when I need it." Emerald backed out of her room. "You're not going to tell on me, are you? I mean, you scratch my back and I'll do yours."

Emerald entered her classroom and smiled at the kids. "Class, we're going to have a drill. You remember what to do in lockdown? I may need you guys to give me a refresher on how to do this, okay?"

Each child simply went to their assigned positions. As chairs were shoved against the doors, some of them started lining up to go into the closets. In less than five minutes her class was ready for whatever happened. Just as she closed herself in with them, she heard the sirens coming closer, and then the explosion of glass being broken. The shit had just hit the fan. Then Nolan yelled for her, and she knew that someone was going to get hurt. She just hoped it was him and not the children.

"Emerald, where the fuck are you?" She closed her eyes and calmed her wolf as Nolan screamed for her. "Come out here and talk to me. I know this is your room. Where the fuck are you? Get your ass on out here right now."

A small hand entered hers, and she held it tightly. Then as the children tightened around her, she knelt down and tried to push them behind her. The door to the closet would only stand so much pounding, as he was doing now, before it caved in. And two punches with something heavy later, he was staring at her with a bat in his hand. He'd broken through the door and was now right in front of her.

The crash of the door to her room happened about the same time Nolan reached into the broken door and touched her. He scraped her face with his nails but didn't touch the children. He turned and ran off when the police entered the room. Emerald hoped they killed the bastard.

~~~

"She's just fine, they said." Jul watched the family as they huddled together and worried over the youngest sister. "Mark said that he'd bring her here personally. She's too upset to drive anyway." He'd just found out that one of the police that had been called to the scene worked for Blair. Or something like that. Jul was having a hard time figuring out what else Blair did that would have hundreds of men and women working for him.

Blair had been the one that received the call from the police about ten minutes ago. Apparently Emerald had been attacked at the school. Jul had missed most of the details, but apparently a boyfriend had gotten upset with her when she'd broken it off and had come to reason with her at the school. A reasoning that had gone bad.

"What sort of classes is she taking that puts her in that sort of harm?" Annabelle looked at him oddly, and he started to tell her that he was just concerned.

"Emerald isn't a student. Oh no. She's a teacher. And she's only at this school to help out over the summer. Some of the students can only pass to the next grade if they take a few more classes. She's helping out the district because they don't have a lot of teachers that are able to work through the summer months." Jul nodded, embarrassed that he'd thought her just a kid. "Emerald is the youngest, but she's in her mid-twenties. Good girl too. And if this man hurt her in anyway, he'll pay. We don't like when someone messes with family."

"I'm sure he will." Jul moved to the deck again when the phone rang. He was sort of uncomfortable at how close this family was. It was great, he knew that, but he'd never had that kind of relationship with anyone other than his parents. When the door behind him opened, he looked at Jade.

"You're freaked out, aren't you?" He shook his head. "Yeah, you are. And I don't blame you. We're a bit much for even our kind."

"Our kind?" She nodded and sat down on the seat that surrounded the deck. "I've been hearing these cryptic things for the past few days. I'm not sure that I'm supposed to understand most of it, but I don't. What do you mean, our kind?"

"I'm not sure what I can tell you. I think we all just assumed because of someone that works for you that you know what we are." Jul sat down and shook his head. "Do you have a secretary or an assistant that works closely with you?"

"Yes. His name is Colby Bass. He's worked for me for years. What does his employment with me have to do with this?" Jade looked out over the field and pool behind the house, and he did as well. The wolf playing in the yard startled him at first, but the longer they watched him, the more he could see that the large dark wolf was having fun.

"What if I told you that the wolf out there is only partly wolf? That the rest of him is human?" She turned to look at him, and he could see that she wasn't kidding. "There are all sorts of us around you all the time. A great many in this house alone. If only you want to take the time to get to know us, you'll know what I'm talking about."

"What do you mean?" He leaned forward in his chair and waited for an answer. She looked at the wolf again, and Jul felt his heart pounding in his chest. He had no idea how much longer he would have waited if not for the car pulling into the drive.

"That would be Emerald. She's going to be very upset when she gets here, so don't take offense if she snaps a little. We're all a bit cranky when we're cornered by a human." When she stood up to leave him, he said her name. "We'll talk more, I promise, but for now I'd like for you to keep an open mind. There are things going on right now that, even if I explained them, you wouldn't understand."

She left him there with that hanging between them. He had no idea, not the slightest clue, what the hell she was talking about, and wondered if he should move out. But as he sat there thinking about all the places he could have been laid up, he saw a man coming out of the woods pulling a shirt over his head. His skin tightened when the man turned to him and waved. It was Allen Henson.

"Boy." Jul nodded. "You enjoying your talk with Jade? She can be a pistol when she needs to be. Sometimes I just pat her on the head and go on about my business. You might want to do that on occasion just until you get used to her."

"She told me that some wolf out there was human too." Allen stared at him for several seconds before he leaned down and pulled his shoes on. Jul watched him tie them up and then lean back in the chair.

"That would be about right," he nodded. Jul had no idea what the fuck was going on, but he felt like he was on one of those shows where they brought out the camera and told you it was all a joke. "She tell you what we were?"

"No. Should she have?" Allen nodded and Jul watched the man pull his sleeve up. "Please don't. I have no idea what you're about to show me, but right now, I don't think I can handle it. I'm...I think I'm slightly freaked out that I'm believing her. I'm not sure what I'm believing, but I'm thinking it's something big."

"You don't want to run when one of us shows you what we are. It might prove to be a little on the dangerous side if you do. We like to chase." Jul stood up and then sat again when Allen told him to. "Just take a few long slow breaths and you'll be just fine. Come on now, breathe."

"What are you?" Jul looked up at Allen when he didn't answer. "Don't show me. Just tell me what you think you are, and I'll nod and believe you."

"Wolf." Of course he was, Jul thought. But he nodded anyway. "I know that you don't believe me and that's okay. But if you work with Blair and Sapphire, they're gonna tell you anyway. No secrets with them two. You're going to be fine as long as you keep breathing, all right?"

"I don't know if I want someone...I can't have...." Jul let out another breath when he started to feel light headed. "You really believe that?"

"I am and I do." Jul stood up again and this time Allen let him. He was making his way to the door when Allen spoke again. "There is no reason for you to be afraid of us. We're not going to harm you in any way." If he'd thought to assure Jul, he'd failed terribly.

Just as Jul was stepping into the doorway, a bundle of a woman came out and hit him full force. As they fell backward onto the decking, he heard her cursing, and was wondering if she would mind teaching him a few of those when he was suddenly airborne. He landed in the pool, the soaking woman right beside him. Good Christ, a sea nymph had just tumbled into his life.

"Don't you fucking watch where you're going?"

Jul wanted to reach out and push the hair from her forehead so he could see what color her eyes were. Right now he'd bet they were sparking off fire, she sounded that pissed off.

"Are you deaf? Where were you going in such a hurry?"

"Into the house. I was trying to get away from Allen." He looked at the deck and noticed how far he was from it. "Did you fly us out here?"

There had to be ten feet between where he'd tried to go in the door to where he was in the pool. Watching the woman get out, her clothing clinging to her skin like it was a part of it, had his cock waking up. He'd not had this kind of reaction to a woman in a very long time.

"Are you on drugs?" He shook his head as he tread water, looking up at her. Jul ran his eyes slowly down her body and felt his entire being charge up. Christ, this was a full package, make you beg kind of woman.

He wanted her, and right now. Her dark nipples were hard against the light fabric of her blouse. The bra she was wearing was lacy, and hid very little from his view. Her belly was flat and looked tone and fit, and her legs, long and muscled, were outlined in the tight dark pants she wore. Jul wondered if she wore matching panties to the bra she had on, and wanted more than anything to find out for himself. But it was her furious face that had him wanting to beg her for a taste of her. She looked like she could tear him apart, and he wanted to see that fire come out when he was between her thighs.

"Are you enjoying what you're looking at?"

Jul grinned. He couldn't help it. She was gorgeous, and he wanted to pull her back into the pool with him and show her just what he was looking at and what it was doing to his body.

"Yes. Very much so. Want to come here and let me show you just how much I am enjoying it?" The laughter from the deck made him remember Allen. He watched the woman as she glared harder at him. Then she looked down at her chest and covered herself up. "Well, that was completely uncalled for. You were making my day. Move your hands and let's have another look before you run off."

Her low growl had him thinking of the big wolf, and he looked into the yard again. When he looked back, not only was she gone, but Allen was standing there with a towel. The old man was laughing as he helped him out of the water.

"You sure do know how to make a first impression." Jul took the towel and dried off. "She's spitting mad right now, and when she calms, she's gonna come gunning for you. Emerald don't take well to people laughing at her."

"She's beautiful. And her anger only made her lovelier." Allen nodded and told him to go on up and change. Dinner would be in about an hour. Nodding, he went to the door just as he thought of something. "You were kidding before, weren't you? About the wolf?"

"Nope." Jul watched him carefully for any sign of insanity. "You go on up now. And get yourself ready. We'll be having a nice talk after dinner." He laughed that special kind of laugh Jul had noticed that Allen had for his grandson Carter, full of humor and fun. "Go on now. Annabelle will be mighty pissed if you're late to dinner. She's looking forward to having all the family at the table tonight."

# Chapter 5

Emerald pulled out pants and a shirt from the drawer. She was so pissed that her head was pounding from it. The nerve of that jerk looking at her like she was naked. Looking down her body, she realized that she almost was and pulled her blouse from her body again. How stupid did she have to be to toss them both into the pool wearing her favorite panty and bra set? When the door opened behind her, she didn't even bother turning, knowing it was one of her sisters.

"I'm fine, for the millionth time. He only tried to break into the school. He didn't hurt any of us." The soft moan had her turning. "What do you think you're doing in here? Get out."

The man had taken his shirt off and it hung limply in his hand. The towel hung loosely over his right side, but otherwise hid nothing from her view. This man had to have been sculpted from marble. And maybe he might have been given an extra dose of sex appeal, because he was reeking of it.

"This is my room." He took a step toward her, and she backed up until her body hit the dresser she'd been going through. "And those are my pants and shirt. Not that I mind you having them on that luscious body, but they are mine. I have an idea...would you like for me to help you undress so you can put them on? Later?"

"You stay back." But of course he didn't. When he was only about a foot from her, she felt her body respond to him as if he were touching her. And when his hand that had the shirt in it stretched toward her, Emerald felt her breath catch. "You don't want to do that."

"Oh, but you're very wrong about that. I want to touch you more than I want to breathe, and I need to do that too." His finger moved along the front of her blouse that she'd opened but not removed. "I was wondering if your panties are the same lacy material as this is."

He slid his finger along the curve of her left breast, then over the right. Her heart was pounding so hard she was sure he could see it. As her blouse draped down over her shoulder where he'd moved it, he leaned in and licked the same path that his fingers had taken. Emerald wanted to pull him closer, but he nipped at her breast and she moaned.

"I've never wanted a woman like I do you. I want to taste every part of you and then take you over and over again until neither of us can move." He made his way up her throat to her mouth and kissed her gently before pressing his body to hers. She felt the thickness of his cock, the length of him as he rocked into her. "Say you want me. Tell me that I can taste you."

"Please." He took her mouth then, ate at her as his tongue danced along her until she was sure there was no part of her mouth that he'd not explored. His hands cupped her ass and she was lifted up, her legs wrapped around him as if it was the most natural thing in the world. They moved then. She had no idea where, nor did she care, but felt the bed touch her as he laid over her. He was rocking to her softness more now, faster and faster, as her body built up for a release.

"Come for me. Let me taste your flesh while you come for me." His fingers pulled and tugged at her nipples, bare now to his touch and gaze. Even as he made his way back down, she knew that the moment he took her into his mouth, the second he bit down on her breast, she was going to come. And when he did it, laving her nipple with his tongue before nipping at her, Emerald covered her mouth with her hand and screamed as she came for him.

Her body was taut with need. Even with the climax he'd given her, she needed more. Her body rolled up to meet his as he rode his hips into her over and over. When he moved down her body, pulling at her pants, Emerald helped him. She needed something from him, and knew that he was going to give it to her. As soon as she lay bare before him, she covered her pussy with her hand and her breast with her arm. He pulled them both away as he looked at her. His face told her he was pleased with what he saw, and her juices heated up for him.

"I'm going to eat you. I have to taste more of you." Emerald nodded and tried not to be embarrassed when he pulled her legs apart and looked at her so intently. "You're so wet. Dripping with need. I want to fuck you, slam deep into your depths, and empty myself into you. But the thought of drinking deeply from you, lapping at your pussy until you fill me, makes me harder than I've ever been."

She didn't want to beg him to do just that, but she might have had he not lowered his head to her pussy and blown over her clit. Emerald moaned and nearly screamed when he took her clit into his mouth and nibbled on her. She was so close to coming right now that if he nipped her again she was going to pass out with it. His fingers entered her then, touched the spot inside of her that no man had ever touched before. Emerald screamed out her release, her body bowing up and falling twice more before she begged him to stop.

He looked down at her as he moved up her body. Reaching between them, Emerald cupped his cock in her hand and watched his face as he rocked into her palm. The thought of him doing the same thing to her body, him moving in and out of her pussy, had her body aching to feel him. The need to have this man take her was making her wolf snarl against her skin. When he lifted his head from her throat, she knew that he'd felt it too.

He looked…afraid. She wanted to reassure him, but his scent hit her. Emerald pulled him closer to her face and inhaled deeply at his neck as she held him. When he lifted his head again and looked down, Emerald knew who he was to her.

"Please get off me." He only stared at her and she shoved him off her. "What the hell do you think you're doing? I don't even know you."

"Julius Whitney. And what was that?" She started to get up off the bed, suddenly embarrassed with her nudity and him being partially clothed. But he pulled her back and she was flat on her back again. He held her hands above her head as he looked down at her. She could see how upset he was, but he was being extremely gentle as he held her. "I asked you a question; what the hell was that just now?"

"The sex? I'm pretty sure you know what it was. And I'm not telling you again to get off me." He rolled to his back and watched her. "I don't want you to touch me again. No matter what."

"Sure thing, lady. But you might want to tell your own body that. You were just as hot to have me as I was you. But at least you got some relief. I'm as hard as stone and want to fuck you." She turned to look at him and could see the budge in his pants. It was mouthwatering to see him lying there that way, his pants undone and his cock, just the tip of it, peeking from the top. While she watched him, he slid his hand over his length, and she moaned when it danced just a little, the fluid at the tip sticking to his skin.

"Come here, Em. Come here and let me take you." Her body responded to the seductive tone and the purr of his voice. She took a step toward him and then another, until she realized what she was doing. "Don't stop. You want me to fuck you as badly as I want to."

"No." He grinned at her and opened his pants more. His cock was bigger than it looked, thicker than she'd imagined, and she wanted him. He stroked his cock, using his own juices as he laid back. The look on his face was one of pure sex, and she wanted to taste him as he had her.

"Ride me."

She wanted to. More than anything, Emerald wanted to slide over him and take her pleasure from him. But he was her mate...she'd almost figured that out too late, but the thought of just running her tongue over him, tasting the creamy juices dripping from him, had her licking her lips.

"I can't." He stood up then, his pants falling to the floor. As he stepped out of them and kept coming toward her, Emerald could only think of one thing, and that was him. But instead of taking her to him, pulling her body to his, he moved to the bathroom and closed the door. As soon as she heard the shower go on, she wondered if he was taking a cold one, because she needed one too.

Grabbing up her clothes, she dressed quickly. Before the water turned off, she was out the door and halfway down the stairs before she thought about what had just happened. Her mate. She had found her mate.

~~~

The water was hurting him, it was so cold. But his cock didn't seem to care how cold it was. Jul knew that the only way he was going to get any relief was to go and find the woman and take her hard. It mattered little to him right now if she was in the bed or the floor. The thought of fucking that woman was making him hurt. Wrapping his hand around his cock, he slowly moved up and down his shaft, thinking about how she'd tasted.

"Christ." He came almost immediately, his cum splashing against the tile wall and dripping down even as he knew that it wasn't going to satisfy him. He was still hard, his balls full of his release as if he'd not just jerked off. Jul fisted his cock again, thinking of the way her breasts had tasted, the way her pussy had felt in his mouth, how tight she was around his fingers, and he thought about her pussy strangling his cock as he came a second, then a third time. He was leaning against the shower wall when he started to laugh.

"What the fuck is wrong with me?"

He had no answer and washed himself up as he stood there thinking. Turning off the water, he dried himself with the thick towel hard enough to redden his skin. The bullet wound had bled a little, but when he pulled off the tape and bandage, he couldn't believe how much it had healed. Jul was coming out of the room when he remembered the way her body had…it had turned into something else.

"Nah, you were just horny. That's it." But he couldn't let it go, couldn't stop thinking about the wolf in the yard, the man who had come out of it. And the woman who had looked like she was on the verge of becoming a wolf as well. Jul was halfway down the stairs when he heard her voice.

"I fucking have no idea what you're talking about. I do not have a mate."

Jul entered the kitchen just as Blair started to speak, and all eyes turned to him. He had never felt so much like a bug pinned to the wall as he did right now. He looked at Allen when he started to laugh.

"You?" Allen was pointing at him and laughing so hard that Jul wanted to turn around and go back to his room. "It's you? Damn boy, you didn't waste any time, now did you?"

Jul felt his face heat up, and he looked at Em. She'd gone pale and he took a step toward her, only to have her back up. When Blair stepped between them, he had the overwhelming urge to hit him out of the way, and took a step back when the feeling seemed to consume him. He'd never felt this way in his entire life about another human being.

"You have any idea what you've done, do you? Or what this all means to you and her?" Again his face heated up and he tried to look away from the imposing man. "Jul, did you have sex with Emerald?"

"Fuck you." Blair stared at him for several second before he turned to Em. She looked like she wanted to murder him and Blair both, but right now he'd do just about anything to have everyone get out so he could find out what the hell was going on.

"You have to tell him." Em shook her head and glared at him. "You can't simply leave this alone, Emerald. You know as well as anyone that it doesn't work that way. You have to tell him what's going on."

"I do not have to tell him a damned thing. And as far as us having sex, it did not happen." He started to tell her she'd had sex while he'd had his with his hand, but he closed his mouth when she looked at him with that glint her eye that told him he was as good as dead if he did. "He and I just kissed, that's all."

Allen snorted and Jul looked at him. There was something in the way they were all treating this that had him walk to Em and pull her into his arms. He'd only meant to hold her, ask her a few questions, but the moment he touched her and she moaned, all bets were off.

She clung to him even as he wrapped his arms around her body. Taking her mouth seemed the most natural thing in the world to him, and he kissed her hungrily, eating at her mouth until he found that he needed all of her. Before he could act on that, pull her up and sit her on the counter, someone touched him from behind and he heard Allen speaking softly.

"You might want to rein that in a tad there, boy. You ain't in the bedroom right now." Jul moaned as he lifted his head. Her taste still lingered on his mouth as he kissed her again. When Allen spoke again, telling him that there was family in the room, Jul could hear his humor, and that made him smile down at the woman in his arms.

"I can't get enough of her. Touching her, tasting her." He didn't look away but he continued talking to Allen. "What's wrong with me that the thought of not having her is making me crazy with lust? And not just crazy, but damned near insane with the need to have her?"

"You're her mate. You know what that is?" Em stiffened in his arms, and he had to hold her tightly or she'd escape again. And right now, the thought of not touching her was making him as crazy as touching her was. Jul wanted her that badly. "Jul? Do you know what it means?"

"Not a clue." He let her pull from him a little, but he didn't let her go. Jul wanted to tell them all to go to hell or anywhere that would leave him time with her, but he needed answers more than he…no, he needed her.

"I'm a wolf." He looked at her, then at the rest of them, hoping for someone to tell him it was a joke. "The least you can do is look at me when I'm talking to you. I said I'm a wolf."

"I've heard this before. I still don't believe it, but Allen told me the same thing." He looked at Blair before continuing. "I suppose you're one too."

"Yes. The head wolf. Alpha." Jul nodded, and he looked at the rest of the people in the large room. "We're all wolves, shifters, or vampires. Sloan and Opal are vamps. We have a panther wolf in our pack, and there are a few other species as well."

"And you all believe this." Blair nodded and Jul felt the air around him seem to heat up. Before he could let her go, Em went from a spitting mad woman to a giant wolf with sharp teeth and claws. He leapt back from her just as her teeth snapped at his chin. "Mother fuck."

She chased him to the door and swiped her paw at him twice before he thought about becoming one with the wall behind him. He glanced over at Allen when he laughed.

"I told you not to run, didn't I? I said when we show you, don't run." Jul would have given anything if Allen would just call her off. "Now you went and pissed off her wolf. The only way to get it out of her system is to let her chase you down. The good news is she won't be able to hurt you."

"But will she be able to kill me?" No one answered him, but Allen did open the back door for him. "What the fuck are you doing? You can't seriously think I'm going to take off running?"

"You wanna see if she can kill you here? This is an awfully tight space here. What if one of her paws accidently swipes your throat and she nicks one of them thick veins there?" Jul eyed the door. "I'll distract her enough for you to get a head start. You get going and run to them trees you seen me playing in, and you might stand a chance."

Allen moved in front of who Jul thought was Em, and Jul took off to the door. He heard a snarl and a laugh, but he was too busy trying to get his feet to get going. As soon as he heard her snarl again, Jul knew he was a dead man. And when her paw swiped at him, he nearly fell but managed to keep going until they were in the trees. Christ, he didn't want to die this way.

He ran until he hurt from it. Jul had no idea where he was, or for that matter, where the big wolf was. He'd about convinced himself that he'd been mistaken when she was standing in front of him. Jul backed so quickly that he fell over a log and had the breath knocked out of him. Before he could get up and get going again, she was over him, her paws on either side of his head.

*You can hear me.* Jul moaned and closed his eyes when he heard Em speaking to him. *Open your eyes and think of me. When you do, you can talk to me.*

All he could think about was her naked, her body slick with sweat from his body. She growled low, and he looked up at her. His body, his cock, was on fire for her. She moved off his body, but not far from him. Jul sat up on his elbows and looked at her as she sat down.

"You're a wolf." The big animal snarled at him and he had to smile. "You do that very well. I'm not sure if I should be afraid or not."

*You should be scared shitless.* He shook his head and sat up on his butt. *Why are you doing this? I mean, I know that we almost had sex, but why did you not leave when I ran away? You'd be safe in a nice hotel in about an hour, and none of this would be happening to you. Why do you still want me?*

"Why do I still want you? Are you...? Christ, woman, have you seen what you look like? You're beautiful." Jul had no idea why, but he thought she didn't believe him. Jul also knew it was more than that, and he wanted her to know. "But it wasn't just that. There was…it was like I was being pulled to you. The need to touch you and to be touched by you was crippling. Then when I did…I guess it wasn't enough just to touch you. I needed you."

*I'm not the kind of person people date.* He frowned at her. *This is…give me your shirt. I'll shift back and we can talk.*

He unbuttoned his shirt and started to hand it to her when it occurred to him what she'd said. "Are you naked? I mean, when you shift, as you call it, are you naked?"

*Is sex all you think of?* He told her it was. *Well, we can't have sex. If we do, it's a done deal. I'll belong to you and to be honest, I've had enough of men trying to own me. I don't care for it.*

She took the shirt when he handed it to her. What she said, what she implied, bothered him. Someone—and he had no idea why he thought so—someone had hurt her. He would bet the bank on it. And a part of him, a part of him he had no idea existed, needed to find this bastard and make him pay.

When she came back from behind the trees, his mouth watered. There wasn't really much of her showing, no more than a pair of shorts and a top would show, but he knew that beneath his shirt, she was bare. He had to swallow twice before he could speak.

"Who is he?" The moment she looked at him, he knew that he'd been right. "This man, are you in love with him?"

"No. God no." She started pacing, and it was doing little to help him concentrate on what they were talking about. "He beat me up. And while I can shift and kill him for it, it's been in public places. Then today, he came to the school. And before you ask me, no, I didn't encourage him in any way."

Jul looked at her and wondered what possessed a person, a man, to hurt another person. Especially a woman. "Does your family know about him? I'm betting that they don't. Because if they did and being what they are, he'd not be around very long. Am I right?"

"No, they don't know about him. And I'd like to keep it that way. They tend to...I'm not a child." He agreed with her, and she turned to frown at him. "I mean, I look like a woman because I'm a full-grown woman. I can think things out, take care of myself. And I have no need for a man to think he needs to be my protector."

"I believe you. But that doesn't mean I don't want to find him and tear his throat out." He grinned at her. "I've never wanted to do that for a woman before. Usually I just nod and let them do whatever they want so long as they...well, you know. It was just a way to get relief. Most of them knew that, and the ones that didn't, I never saw again. Then things heated up at work and I didn't have time for women. Or sex."

"I've never had sex before." He looked at her hard. There was no way that she was a virgin. "I have been...I have vibrators, but I never used them inside of me. I just...they were a way to relieve some tension, like you said. After being with you, I can tell you that they paled in comparison."

His cock ached to show her how much more could be done to relax her. He thought of her naked, under him and screaming out his name. When she shivered her nipples hardened, and her body swayed enough that he knew she was thinking of him too. Jul wanted to have her come in his mouth again. He wanted to fuck her hard enough to have her scream out his name. Jul reached down and cupped his aching cock and balls.

"Come here, Em. I want to taste you again." She shook her head, but took a step toward him. "I love the way your juices slide down my throat, the way your clit hardens when I touch it, suckle at it. I want to drink from you until I'm satisfied. Which won't be any time soon."

Another step toward him brought her close enough to touch. Jul ran his hand up her leg to her apex. She was wet, and her juices slid over his fingers as he played with her curls. Pulling her gently, she moved closer, close enough that he could lift the shirt enough to see her bounty.

Turning her so that he could drink from her, he cupped her ass and licked her nether lips. Her moan encouraged him enough to nibble on her before he sucked her clit into his mouth and his tongue into her sheath. With her riding his mouth now, he reached down with his hand and freed his cock. He ached to be inside of her, but he wanted to give her pleasure first. Her hand on his head had him pulling her closer still, and he feasted on her as she rode his mouth.

Her scream had him fisting his cock. Christ, to be inside of her, fucking her hard and fast. As she rode his mouth, he felt his balls tighten up and he knew that he was going to come. When she stepped back from him, Jul could only stare at her.

"What do I do?" He had no idea what she was talking about, and when she dropped to the ground beside him and wrapped her hand around his, he leaned back. "I want to taste you. I need to...tell me what to do."

"If you put your mouth over my cock, I'm going to come. And hard." She nodded and leaned down, but he pulled her up before she touched him. "I want to fuck you. I want to be buried deep inside of you and release. Please."

Her nod sent him over the edge of reason. Rolling her to the ground, he tore his shirt open and took her breast into his mouth. His need was consuming him, and he fisted his cock to slide into her when she put her hand on his heart.

"Take me." He seemed to calm then at her voice. Jul watched her face as he slowly entered her, her heat and juices making his cock fit her despite his size. When he felt her maidenhead, the barrier that told him she was his, he kissed her and slammed forward. When she screamed, he emptied himself in her. There was no hope for anything else. But when she licked his shoulder and bit him, he surged forward again and again until he came again, this time bringing her with him.

# Chapter 6

Sloan was sitting in her kitchen when she got home. Jul was still at the house with his mother and her family, and she was glad for that. Emerald wanted some time alone, and he seemed to understand that. But Sloan being here scared her just a little.

"It didn't go well." Emerald sat down. The little boy and his father. "I tried to...he wasn't the only one hurting him. They were both...did you know that they were having sex with him?"

"No. I only saw the bruises and what they did to him where I could see it." Sloan got up to pace. "Sloan, where is the little boy? I know you didn't hurt him. Where is he now?"

"I'm so sorry, honey. I was too late. He was dead when I got there. I had...they were still having sex with him. I don't think they realized what they'd done to that point. And that made me...." He paced for several more turns before he sat down again. "I killed them both. My rage was so out of control that I killed them both before I could gather my wits about me. There was another child, the little girl that you told me about. I took her to the hospital. It did not look good for her either. So I helped her a little."

She went to her cabinet and pulled down a bottle of bourbon. Emerald was glad it was Saturday or she might have gone to work with liquor on her breath. But right now, she needed this more than she needed a job.

"He wanted to stay at the school last night. Do you suppose he knew what was going to happen to him when he went home?" She took a burning gulp of the fiery liquid. "I should have brought him with me. Or called the police. I'm not supposed to, but I should have."

"Had you done anything to help him temporarily, it would only have happened again and again later." She nodded. Knowing that didn't really help her. "Emerald, the little girl, she is going to need care. More than any human can give her. Someone needs to step in and take her before she is lost in the system. You need to bring her to this family."

"Me?" He nodded. "I have no idea how to care for a kid. I mean, I teach them, but to have one full time? I haven't any idea what to do. And if she needs help like you said, then I'm not sure how to give it to her. I failed her brother. What makes you think I can do anything good for her?"

"You have a mate. And with him you can do so much for her." She flushed and he smiled. "You will be able to care for her in ways that no one else can. And her brother would like to know that you have her."

Emotional blackmail. That was what he was doing, plain and simple. "Why don't you take her in? You and Opal have a house and money."

"We're vampires." She knew that, but to hear him say it brought home the problems they might encounter when their own child was born. He smiled at her unspoken concern and answered her. "We're making arrangements. There will be someone with the child at all times when we cannot be. And Opal is a day person. She will be able to be there more than me."

"I can't take this child, Sloan. I don't even know how to care for myself." He looked around the room and she did as well. It was a small apartment. One bedroom, a living room/kitchen/dining room combined, and a bath. That was it. And if you counted the closet, the single closet, she had a total of four rooms to keep herself in. "In a few weeks I'm going to be homeless too. This place is being renovated as condos, and I can't afford it. And if you suggest I have my mate take me in, I'll stake you where you sleep."

"But it's all true. He needs to care for you. Jul has money. A great deal of it. I'm assuming that he will purchase the two of you a home." She told him that they'd not talked long term for now. "He will need to see to your needs, Emerald. Have you even told him about your housing situation? Have you told anyone?"

"No, and I won't, either. I can see to my own needs, thanks." She didn't have any idea why that bothered her so much, but it did. "I have to get some things done around here. So if you don't mind leaving me to it, I'd very much appreciate it."

Sloan stared at her for several seconds before he stood up. He was a big man, imposing, and she backed up several steps, shielding her face with her arms. When he frowned at her, she wanted to tell him it was habit, but he seemed to know.

"This other man, he's been here before. Recently. Are you aware of that?" She shook her head. "You will need to be careful. There is the scent of death about him. He is dangerous, isn't he?"

"Yes." He asked her if she'd told Jul. "No. I think he thinks there is someone else, but not…how did you know?"

"You are one I would rarely consider afraid of much. You have been…lately I have noticed that you are afraid of your own shadow. When one of the men stand, you move away. And recently you seem to be away more than ever. Are you thinking that you can protect us from him, or are you hiding what he's done to you?"

She wasn't sure how to answer him. Or even if she wanted to. "He's not anyone I dated really. I never even went out with him. I…he just latched onto me and I can't get rid of him. And now he's hurting the people I meet or know. I was with a friend of mine, and this guy shows up and acts like we're more than we are. More than we'd ever be. He told my date what he and I were married. He keeps showing up. Threatening me. He came to the school, too."

"You need to tell your family, all of it." She nodded but said nothing. "And you must find a more secure place to live. He has been in here. I thought…I had no idea that it wasn't the two of you in your bed."

She looked at him and then made her way to the other room. She stopped in the doorway and could smell him there. And if that didn't let her know he'd been there, then the bed would have. He'd been in it, and even from where she stood, she detected the stench of sex and of bowel movement. Emerald felt rather than saw Sloan behind her. This was just too much.

"He's insane. I don't mean in a way that makes you think that he's funny, but nuts insane. But as of now I have nowhere to go that won't put the family in harm's way. This guy is dangerous, and there are little ones at the house." Sloan said again that this place was unsafe. "I'll talk to Blair and Sapphire. But...I know it's late, but can you stay while I pack a few things?"

"No. You know that I cannot. Just a moment." He disappeared and she moved into her room. There was little here that she wanted or needed right now, and the thought that Nolan might have touched them made her skin crawl. Seeing a man standing in her doorway made her scream, but then he said her name.

"Em, it's me." She fell into Jul's arms. Sobbing now, she let him hold her as she told him everything. "Come on, baby. Let me take you somewhere else. What do you need?"

"I can't touch this stuff. All my things, he's been here. He's touched them." He nodded as if he understood. Holding her, he took her to the kitchen and sat her in the chair. That's when she noticed that not only was his shirt all buttoned up wrong, but his hair was wet. She ran her finger over his wet curls.

"I was in the shower and this giant hulking man comes in, throws back the curtain, and tells me that I have to come with him now. Then as I'm drying off, while he's standing there mind you, he tells me that someone had violated your space. Who talks like that?" She smiled at him as he sat in the chair across from her, not letting go of her hand. "Then as I'm getting dressed, he tells me that a man you don't know all that well has been here, and that if I don't provide you a safe place, he will and will take it out of my hide. He is one scary fucker."

"He is. And extremely protective of us. He thinks we're...the women...are helpless." Jul kissed the back of her hand. "I'm okay now if you want to go back to the house. I'm going to pack a few things up and go to a hotel or something."

"I don't think so. First of all, I have to provide you a place to stay. Strict orders. Secondly, where you go I go from now on. I'm not sure when that sort of thinking entered my head, but I like it. And you." He stood up and looked around. "I think my first car was bigger than this place. How can you live in such a tight place?"

"It was cheap. And on a teacher's salary, it was all I could afford." She looked around the room and could see that many of her things had been moved, and she shivered again. "I'm not sure I can ever stay here again, cheap or not."

"I don't want you to." She looked at him and he sat back down. "I had a long talk with Annabelle and my mom this morning. I had no idea that my...my mother knew about shifters her whole life. And when I asked her why she didn't say anything, she said she assumed that with Colby working for me, I knew. I had no idea he was a wolf too."

"You smell like him. Not as much as you did when you first got here, but I could smell him." Jul leaned back in the chair. "What did you learn besides your mom is more hip to us than you?"

"That we're mated and bonded. That nothing can tear us apart. I have no idea how I feel about that, but I do know that keeping you safe is all I can think about." She got up and put the alcohol away and rinsed the glass out. "What are you thinking, Em?"

"I have no idea what to think. A man I barely know and hate was in my house. He...he did things on my bed that should never have happened. Then he touched my things. No less a violation but still, that's what he did. And now I've a mate, no home, no money to speak of. A vampire that thinks a child that was raped by her parents will be better off with me, and a dead little boy that I feel responsible for." He turned her around and she looked at him. "I'm a wolf, a big predator that shouldn't be afraid of anything, and there's a man out there that is stalking me, and all I can think about is taking you somewhere and letting you hold me."

He moved them to the door. She went with him knowing that whatever was on the other side of the door was going to be fucked if they messed with her now. Before she could think about where they might be going, a long black limo pulled up and the driver was out before they were near the thing. As he opened the door, he nodded once to them and looked around. Emerald had a feeling that this man would take a bullet for Jul.

Emerald curled around his body as soon as they were both in the back. She let Jul hold her in a way that no one had before and, as they were mates for life, no one ever would again. She closed her eyes, wondering if they could stay this way forever as he spoke to someone. When he lifted her chin up, she looked at him and fell head over heels in love.

"We're going to a hotel. Do you need anything before we get there?" She told him she had nothing. "Good. I'm having Tayler take us to the mall. We'll get what we need there."

She nodded and leaned into him again. As he made calls, talking to Colby and a woman by the name of Mrs. Donald, she let the last few days drift away and let sleep claim her.

~~~

Jul had never been one to shop. When he needed clothing, he had someone shop for it for him, or he had a man come to his office and measure him for whatever he needed. At his apartment back home, he had about two dozen suits, several dozen shirts, and he didn't even want to think how many ties he had. But shopping in the mall with Em had to be the best time he'd ever had. She was in the dressing room again when his phone rang. Mrs. Donald launched right into what she wanted him to know.

"There are any number of houses on the market near the address you gave me. Three of them have the requirements you requested, and one can be set up that way. However, one of the three is much larger. Bigger than you asked for." Jul watched the door as he asked the realtor how big. "Fourteen bedrooms, eleven baths, and a dining room that can hold up to fifty guests comfortably. There is also a kitchen in the sublevels that will literally feed an army of guests. Olympic pool with pool house, a cook's house with three bedrooms, a seven car garage, as well as a stable for horses. Which I might add can be purchased with the house. The owners are getting rid of everything. Furniture as well."

"And the security?" She told him as of right now there was a fence surrounding the five hundred acres that the house set on, but the rest of the land, all twelve hundred acres, were open. "What's the offer?"

"They are desperate to sell. I've not found out why as yet, but desperate. The asking amount is cheap, but I think you can go lower. I can set you an appointment to see the house anytime you want." He told her today, in an hour if possible. "I can do that. Like I said, they want this gone from their lives. And Mr. Whitney, you should also be aware that the house is reputed to belong to vampires."

Jul looked up just as the dressing room curtain opened. His breath caught and he could only stare at Em. Christ. She was gorgeous.

"Set it up for an hour. Meet us there if you can. Send the address to my phone." She told him she would, and he closed the connection. He moved to Em slowly. "You have to have this one too."

Her laughter made his body hum. It was free and happy, things that he wondered if she'd had in a while. "You've said that about everything I've tried on. I can't look that good in everything. And all I really needed was a pair of pajamas and some under things. You're spending much too much as it is."

Instead of answering her, he turned her to look at the full length mirrors behind her. There were three of them, and he stepped up behind her and wrapped his arms around her tiny waist. He wanted to lay her over the closest chair and have his way with her.

"Do you know what I see? A sexy, vibrant woman who takes my breath away. My heart skips beats when you come near me." He cupped her breasts in his hands and loved how they filled them. "You're gorgeous. And it's all I can do not to bend you over right now and take you. Make you scream out my name while I eat you. Christ, I can't seem to get enough of you."

He had no idea what they might have done had the clerk that had been hovering around them not cleared her throat. Em had told him she was a wolf too, and a part of Ruby and Josh's new pack. Her smile told him that she knew just what they were thinking.

"I can have it put with the rest of your things unless you want to wear it home." Jul nodded. "Good choice. I've always thought that Emerald looked good in that color blue. It matches your eyes, too."

When she walked away, he pulled Em into his arms and kissed her. It would have to do for now as they had to get moving. But when she moaned, he cupped her ass and rocked into her. Stepping back from her was the hardest thing he'd ever done.

"We have an appointment." She looked dazed and he laughed. "That is a good look on my Miss Erickson. It makes you look sexy and wanton. A look that I could get used to very quickly."

"You do know that I'm paying you back for all this. Every bit of it." She looked at the price tag on the dress and then back at him. "Okay, it'll take me about ninety years, but I'll get it paid."

"You really want to pay me back?" She nodded and he grinned. "Then come with me and enjoy what we're doing. And don't say no until you hear me out."

"I'm not going to like this, am I?" He told her probably not. "Then why are we doing it? If you know that I'm going to be upset, why are you doing it?"

"I need to keep you safe." She didn't say anything as he settled the bill. Tayler helped carry their purchases out to the waiting limo and then winked at him when he handed Em into the car. He didn't think he'd ever seen him do that before. And he paused to ask him what he thought of his Em.

"She's a keeper. But I think you already figured that out, didn't you?" Jul nodded. "You know what she is? Besides the best thing that will ever happen to you?"

"My mate. A wolf. A school teacher." Tayler smiled and nodded as he went to the other side of the car to open the door for him. "What are you?"

"Tiger." Jul nodded. "Mr. Whitney? This woman, she's in trouble? You called me here because she's in trouble, didn't you?"

"Yes. A man is stalking her, and I fear for her life. I know that she's a wolf, a very capable one at that, but he's dangerous and scary. I need you to help me keep her safe." Tayler nodded and told him he would. "I thank you. And Tayler, I'm going to move here. Do you have a problem with that? Can you see yourself moving here?"

"To work for you, Mr. Whitney, I'd live about anywhere. And the missus there, she's about the prettiest thing I've ever seen." Then he laughed. "And she's got you all twisted up. It looks good on you."

Jul got into the limo and pulled her into his arms. Yeah, he wanted to tell Tayler, it felt pretty good too. As she talked about the clothing they'd gotten, he thought about living with her for the rest of his life, and for some reason, it didn't scare him like it normally did when a woman got too close.

The gates to the house were opened. As they drove through them, she looked at him but said nothing. He'd reminded her again that she had to listen to him first before getting upset. The moment the house came into view, however, he knew that not only did she love it, but he felt as if he were home.

"The owners have gone out for the evening," Mrs. Donald told him in way of greeting. "They have said if you have any questions, we can call them, but they wanted you to see it as if it were yours. The staff, if you would like, have said that they would stay on if you want them to."

"Staff?" He winked at Em when she sounded panicky. "I know that I'm not supposed to say anything, but this house is monstrous. You can see that, right?"

"Yes." He kissed her mouth. "Keep an open mind and we'll look the house over. Then at the end you can tell me what you don't like about it."

She looked like she might hit him, but she turned and walked up the steps. Jul stood watching her until the realtor cleared her throat. Then Jul moved up the stairs as well and entered what he knew was going to be his first home.

The house was perfect. The furniture matched each room as if it had been designed with the room in mind, which Jul thought it had. The kitchen was as he had imagined it being, large and open, white tile, with every kind of equipment needed to serve a houseful. He did have a thought about the vampires living there, but was told without asking that they entertained a great deal. The cook in the kitchen told him that she'd be available to stay if he should want her to.

The dining room was massive but could be made into something for a smaller group with the closing of a few doors, the butler told him. There was china in all the wall units that looked like it was seasonal, and Jul watched as Em walked around to each of them with her hands behind her back. Jul thought about having his mom and Em's family over at Christmas time and smiled.

As they were led up to the third and fourth floors, he watched Em as she touched things here and there, straightened a pillow that had looked good to him, and smiled a great deal. They were in the master bedroom, a place he could have put his entire winery in, when he finally asked her what she thought.

"You know what I think. I love this place." She turned from looking out over the pool at him. "Why are we looking at this? You're not thinking of buying it, are you?"

"I am going to buy it." She turned and looked out the window. "I won't if you don't want me to. But I can tell that you love this place. So do I. And I can see us having our families here for holidays, the pool in the back filled with everyone while we have a big dinner out of doors. And there is enough land for you to run on as well. Lots of it."

"I'm not used to the kind of wealth you have." He understood that. Jul had grown up with lots of money and the things it brought to his life. But he could also see what a person on the outside might think of his kind of rich. "You are very rich, aren't you?"

"Very." He didn't know what to say to her when she was quiet like this. "Em, I'm not sure if you believe me right now, but I want to share this with you. I would love to live here with you, and have babies, our babies, grow up here. I know you like this place. I can see it in your face, but if it's too much, we can look more."

"I love this place, like you said, but...." She turned again, this time wrapping her arms around his neck. "This is so fast. How long have we known each other? A week? Ten days? Don't you think this is sort of scary fast?"

He loved her. Just in that moment, Jul knew that he was in love with her, and the amount of time they'd known each other mattered little. Christ, he was in love with Emerald Erickson. Going down on one knee, he held her hand. When she struggled just a little, he kissed the back of her wrist and looked up at her.

"I have no ring to give you. But I do have my heart. And I give it to you freely. I've never been in love before, never thought it even possible that I'd find someone, anyone, that would make me feel like you do. I love you. A declaration that I have never said to a woman in my life, but to you I say it over and over. I love you, Em. With all my heart, I love you. And if you would do me the honor of being my wife, I'll show you every day how much I love you." He kissed her hand again and looked up at her face. She was crying and nodding. Jul stood up and pulled her into his arms and kissed her again, this time with all the love he could give her. When he lifted his head from hers, she smiled at him.

"Can I buy you this house?" She nodded again. "Good. And will you help me fill the rooms, all of them, with family? Children of our own, others if you want?"

"Yes." He kissed her again. "But we have to take care of Nolan first. He's not going to ruin this for us."

"He won't." As they went to find Mrs. Donald, Jul thought of all the things he was working on to insure that Bruce didn't ruin anyone's lives again, especially those of his new family.

# Chapter 7

Nolan pulled his book out again. He was still trying to finish off the bitch, Winter, but she had more guards around her room than he'd seen anywhere else. And the man? He had no fucking clue where they'd taken him, but he was gone. Maybe he was dead, but Nolan scoured the paper every day and had not read a single thing about him. As he put this notebook away, he pulled out the cash and jewelry he'd collected today. It had been a terrible day for him, and just looking at the things he did manage to get didn't make it any better.

The cable company he was working for had no fucking clue what went on when they assigned them a job. He didn't really work for the cable company itself, but was a contractor for them. He did the installs. And he also, when the mood was on him, did a few pick-ups as well. Like the pretty little bracelet he'd gotten today on his first run.

The first place he'd had a woman that was so fucking ugly that he'd nearly told her that he had another call. But she was wearing this diamond on her finger that looked like it would choke a horse. So he went in and wired her house up. He'd also managed to get over three hundred bucks in cash that was laying on the bedside table, a watch that had three faces on it, as well as a nice little bottle of muscle relaxers for his trouble. But the next house he went to nearly got him caught at his fucking around.

He knew the moment that she opened the door that she wanted him. Her body screamed at him to take her, and the short little skirt she had on...well damn, it was fine. As she told him where she wanted each cable unit installed, he walked behind her, watching her ass swing back and forth. She'd nearly caught him twice, but he'd been at this game a lot longer than she had, and he managed to pretend to look at anything else when she turned in his direction. As soon as she led him to the bedroom, Nolan made his move.

"You wanna fuck?" She eyed him carefully and told him to show her his cock. It wasn't really what she'd said, but he could see it in her eyes. Freeing his cock, he fisted himself as she stood there. Christ, she was going to be a screamer, Nolan knew it. He popped her in the head when she turned her back to him, as if she was begging him to do it, and he knew that she was going to be so much fun.

Throwing her to the bed, like he knew she'd love, he held her down while he used his tape on her. Nolan took her picture with his cell phone and emailed it to himself. Then he deleted it from his phone as he looked down at her. She'd been begging him with her eyes, and he was hard as stone watching her. When he had her taped to the bed at all four corners, he cut away her clothing with his box knife.

"Yeah, you want this." He stroked his cock again as he watched her. "And I'm going to give it to you as soon as I get you ready."

As he cut into her leg, the blood poured from the wound. He ran his hands all through it as he got harder and harder, his cock aching to come. As soon as he was covered in it, he fisted his cock again and felt his balls tighten up. Before he came, however, he reached into his pocket and pulled on a condom.

"We don't want any little surprises now, do we?" As soon as he had it fitted over him, he fisted his cock again. This time he held his balls tightly as he watched the blood pour from her.

Nolan came twice while she was tied up. He knew that she'd want some sort of relief too, but he was making her wait for a bit. Women liked that kind of shit with him, and he kind of enjoyed it himself. After disposing of the used condom by flushing the commode three times, he turned on the shower and stepped in.

After he cleaned with a hot shower, he opened the bathroom medicine cabinet to have a looksee while he dried off. He'd found the prescription almost as soon as he opened it. The clear bottle and the syringes were laying on the bottom shelf.

"Anticoagulant. U F Heparin," he read aloud. "Take three times daily." He looked at the back of the bottle, and it had all kinds of warnings on it. Test. If bleeding is profuse, call nine-one-one. Nolan walked back into the bedroom to see what profuse might mean to her, and was surprised to see that she wasn't breathing. Nolan went into panic mode.

It wasn't as if he wasn't going to kill her anyway. That was his plan all along. But the fact that she'd died before he'd had his fun and that she'd bled out without him having any say in it had given him a scare. Not a big one, but enough to throw him off his game. He'd panicked, and that was what nearly got him fucked up.

Calling the police was out of the question. They'd be there before he got a chance to clean up, and there was no fucking way he could do this quickly. As he began gathering his things — tape, box knife, and a couple of other things he'd used on her — he congratulated himself on parking on the street over from this one. It was a habit he'd been doing for years. He was pulling the tape off when he thought of the residue it might leave.

"Think." He sat down and took several deep breaths. He had to be calm or like the people who got caught, he'd be in jail in a matter of minutes. Nolan reached for his bag of tools and counted them. Realizing that he was missing one, he searched everywhere. He found it still in the bed with the woman. She'd been playing with it the entire time, he knew it.

Then he went to the bathroom. He'd been wearing gloves, of course, but he still wiped things down. Putting the bottle back on the shelf, he flushed the toilet three more times to make sure that the condom was gone as well. He had heard about things being taken from the toilet and getting some of his fellow cohorts caught. This was not going to be his downfall.

The bedroom was a little trickier. Nolan went to the door twice and walked in the way they had to see what he might have touched. Nothing but her. And that had only been to help her on the bed, then tie her down. Taking out the alcohol pads he used to wipe over surfaces before sticking anything to it, he wiped her arms down, and her ankles. As he finished with each pad, he made sure he put it into the zip bag he'd brought. Calming now, he left the bedroom and went down the hall to the front door, counting his tools again as he went. Everything was there. But things were not as they had been left by him and the woman.

The front door had not been touched by him, not even to open the door. Another habit he'd gotten into. He never wanted any of the bitches to come back on him saying that he'd forced his way in. As he moved to the door, he noticed almost immediately that he was in deeper shit than he'd thought. The door was open just a little.

Then he had heard a sound in the kitchen...a man humming. Nolan nearly screamed when the little dog that he'd seen when he came in came walking toward him. The low growl from the little dog made his heart rate leap up, and he had nearly gone into a panic again. Nolan ran to the door, pushed it open with the screwdriver he had in his hand, and went out. Just as the door started to latch shut, he saw the man going up the stairs. Nolan had left by rounding the house and going to his truck.

And now here he was, at home and still a little freaked out about what had happened. Not killing the woman, hell no. Had she not wanted him to fuck her and then kill her, she shouldn't have been there where he could. It wasn't crazy talking, but the truth. Women set themselves up to be hurt by him. Begged him to, he thought with a grin.

Opening his book to the first blank page, he took it to his computer. Printing out the picture on his email, he deleted it from his email, then his trashcan. No one would be able to take his computer and frame him for shit that wasn't there. After securing the photo in his notebook, he got out his paperwork and copies of the paperwork, and wrote down her name. "Margaret Hansel, thank you very much." She only got two stars because she'd let herself be dead too soon, as far as he was concerned. Still, it was a good release for him. Nolan closed his eyes and let himself rest for a while.

When he woke it was dark. Stretching, he sat there and thought about how amazing he felt. Turning on the news, he went into his kitchen and got out four of the many frozen dinners he had, and popped them in the microwave. The part where Mrs. Hansel had been found by her husband today was just coming on.

"Mr. Hansel, a well-respected and dedicated husband, came home today to find his wife brutally murdered." Nolan took offense to that. He didn't do nothing more than tie her up and cut her one time. Brutal was what he did to bitches that fucked him over. Like that Winter bitch and Erickson. He was really going to be brutal to them as soon as he found them.

He barely listened as they went on and on about how she was a lovely woman. How she had volunteered at the homeless shelter twice a week. And that she'd been on the way to have her heart transplant in a couple of days. Instead, he tried to think how to get to that fucking Erickson bitch. She had been on his list for far too long.

He had gone back to the school over the weekend to tell her that she was going to finish what they'd started, completely forgetting it was Saturday. Then on Monday, today, he'd gone by on his way to work, and was blocked entrance to the area. The mall cop, or whatever the hell he was, had said that unless he had a good reason for being there, he wasn't to come on the property. As much as he wanted to point out that his taxes being paid to have that place even open was enough to let him go where the fuck he wanted, he didn't want the cop to remember him. So instead he asked him about an address, saying that's all he wanted anyway. Nolan turned off the television just as a blurry video came on.

Going through his notebook, he found Erickson's address again. He was headed out the door when he remembered that he had to put things back. Shoving the notebook back under the floor, he smiled to himself. He was the perfect killer. Nolan thought that they might even do a movie of the week about him someday. But they'd have to leave things open. There was no way they were ever going to catch him. And the ending would just have to be open.

Driving to her little place, he thought of her. Emerald Erickson was prime. Her tits were a nice handful, and her body fit against his like they'd been made to go together. Fucking her, if he ever wanted to, would be epic. He could almost feel himself coming with her several times as he took her. Damn, but she'd make his cock so hard, like it was right now he realized, that he'd have to fuck her seven or eight times a day just to get his rocks off. Nolan could not wait to find the bitch and have her take up where they'd left off.

~~~

"I've been by your place." Emerald looked up at the only other teacher that had come to work today. Out of the four of them that she'd been told would be working with her, one had never shown up and her class had to be divided into the rest of their classes, and the woman who'd not come in today hadn't even called to say she wasn't going to be in.

"What place is that?" She'd not told anyone about her and Jul buying a house. Hell, she'd not even told her family just where it was yet. Just that she and Jul had decided to try this thing out, and that they'd purchased a home.

"That place where your family lives. Some major goings on there. What are you doing? Having the place renovated?" To be honest, Emerald had no idea what was going on at her sister's house. She was there over the weekend, but hadn't noticed anything going on. "Last year you had all the trees brought in, and now you're having something big done. What is it?"

"I don't know. I don't live there, my sister and her husband do." Emerald sipped her water. "Why were you out that way? I didn't think anything was out near their place."

"I was out with my boyfriend and I knew where you lived." *That's creepy*, Emerald thought, but said nothing. "There was all these signs about no trespassing, but we didn't think anyone would care if we just peeked."

"I'm pretty sure that's what no trespassing means, no peeking." The teacher huffed at her. Emerald knew her last name was Fletcher, and that only because she had a sign outside her door that proclaimed all that came through her doors were Fletcher children. Whatever that meant.

"It's not like anyone really cares about that. I bet your sister and her family enjoy having people come up and look at their home." Emerald told her no, they didn't. "Oh come on. Someone with that kind of money to spend only does that to show off. And if things get out of hand sometimes, they can say that the signs were posted when the cops come by to take away someone who's gotten out of hand. We didn't, but there are some who might."

"I'm pretty sure that my family likes their privacy. So if I were you, I'd stay out the next time. She won't like to have to call the police on you. And believe me, she will." Fletcher huffed again and left her at the table. The kids were due in at nine and it was ten minutes till. As she made her way to the classroom, she wondered who was caring for the other class. But the room was empty of anyone, so Emerald went to her own room.

Two more weeks and she'd be done with this. And after that she had a month before the pack school reopened. According to Blair, there was going to be a whole new set of students to come to them this year as well. After thinking about it for about ten seconds, she decided that she was not going to sub in this district again. Not for the summer or even when she was off. There was just too much stress in this place.

As the kids started to come into the room, Emerald noticed that most of them were quiet. The day before she'd told them about Connor and that he'd been hurt very badly. She wouldn't tell a bunch of eight and nine year olds that he'd been killed no matter what they heard at home. Connor's sister, Katie, was still in the hospital, but doing well now. She had talked to Jul about her, but never asked him about taking her in. She still wasn't sure about that.

Getting them settled took an extra five minutes today. No one, it seemed, could focus. As she handed out the muffins she'd picked up on the way in, she thought about what Jul had told her as she left for work.

"Don't go out unless you can see Tayler. He's going to be hanging around you all day, but in the shadows. I'm not sure what that means to him, but he said you'd be able to see him when nobody else can." She nodded. "You understand, don't you?"

"Yes. I can smell him." Jul nodded and then smiled. "Yes, before you ask, I can smell you too. You have a scent about you that makes my wolf hum with happiness, if you want to know the truth. Why is all this so much fun to you?"

"To find out the amazing things you can do? I don't have a clue. But it is. Just knowing that you can go into heat and that anyone around you can smell that we've had sex makes me feel like king of the mountain. Who knew?" She wanted to brain him. "When you get home tonight, I'm going to hide in the woods and you can shift and come looking for me again. Then if you find me quick enough, I'll let you have your way with me. If you don't, then I'll have my way with you." With a quick kiss, he left her. She was still standing in the hall when Tayler came to get her.

Now she knew that Tayler was around, he'd been in to see her twice but he never said anything. When she was finished handing out the small bottles of juice that had been on her desk, she looked up just as he entered her room.

"I just wanted to let the kids know that I'm the new janitor." The kids looked at him like they had no idea what a janitor was. "I'll be working around the rooms today too. You all just go on like you don't see me."

"What's your name?" Emerald glanced at Timmy as he stood up to Tayler. "We're not supposed to talk to strangers. So if you tell us your name, we don't have to be a scared of you."

"It's Tayler. I'm just plain old Tayler." He moved to her desk and she saw him put something on it. Then he picked up her trashcan and took it out. As she made her way back to the desk, he returned a different can to her. With a quick nod, he was gone again.

As the children enjoyed their snack, she opened the thick envelope. Out of it fell a small cell phone and a note. She held the phone while she read the note.

*There's a tracker in this, so try and keep it on you at all times. I know that we can talk whenever we want, but that doesn't help Tayler.* Emerald looked out the window and saw the man in question walk the play yard. She went back to the note. *There's a camera in the trashcan. He said that he can see the entire room, but that he'd very much prefer that he didn't block it by putting it under your desk. I also wanted to tell you that I love you very much and will see you tonight. Love Jul.*

"Stupid man." But she was smiling as she thought of how much effort he was putting into keeping her safe. Emerald really did feel better knowing that someone was there to help her in the event that Nolan returned.

Mr. Basel was her helper today. He helped the kids cut out circles, a difficult thing for most children at this age, while she went over the writing sheets they'd done yesterday. They were getting much better, and she'd even taken out her stickers and was putting them on the sheets when she felt someone standing next to her. Emerald nearly jumped out of her skin when she turned and saw Opal there.

"You scared me." The children laughed, and she told them to work quietly please. When she looked at her sister, she knew something had gone wrong. "What is it? The baby?"

"You have to go downtown with Sapphire. There is something that the police want you to look at." Emerald nodded. "You have to take a breath, honey, or you'll pass out."

"Is it Jul? Has something happened to him?" Opal told her no, that he was going to meet her at the station. "Then what is it? Tell me."

"There was a murder yesterday. A woman was killed in her home, and the police have a video of the person they think did it. They want you to come down and see if you can identify him." She asked why her. "Because in addition to that murder, they think the same man broke into your apartment again. This time...oh honey, this time he killed your neighbor, Mrs. Grosshandler."

Emerald stood up then sat again. The little lady was the sweetest thing in the world. Nosey as hell, but sweet. Nodding, she stood up and gathered her things. She looked around the room just as her sister continued.

"I'm going to sub for you. I've already made sure that no one will say a word about it." Emerald nodded. Her sister could do a lot of things now thanks to Ursula. "And I've already spoken to Tayler. He's going to take you."

"What about you? I can't leave you here alone." Opal nodded to the door, and she saw Sloan and Quentin there. "I still don't want you hurt. He's dangerous if it's him that killed that woman, and I don't feel right leaving you here."

"I'm going to be fine. I swear." Tayler came into the room, and she found herself being put into the limo that had brought her in. She was numb, and when she felt Jul touch her mind she nearly sobbed with relief.

*I'm here at the station waiting. Blair is here, as well as Sapphire and your grandmother.* She told him that she and Tayler were on their way. *I'm here, baby. I'm not leaving you.*

*He killed that poor little woman. And that other one. What is wrong with him?* He told her he had no idea, but with her help they might be closer to catching him. *I don't know what they expect me to see that they didn't.*

*Blair told them about your apartment being broken into before. The sheets that he used are in evidence now. And they have a surveillance camera outside the house of the woman that was killed that they want you to look at. It's not good, but you might be able to tell them better than anyone if it's Bruce or not.*

As soon as she arrived, she was taken to a large room. Jul was there as well as Sapphire, but Blair and her grandmother were not. When she asked, Sapphire laughed. This could not be good.

"Grandmother decided that you were not going to be treated like a common criminal. She put up a fuss, and now she and Blair are getting a talking to." She asked what he'd done. "He was defending her honor, of course."

"Of course."

Jul held her hand while they waited, and when two people, a woman and a man, came in, Emerald knew that she was a wolf. At her smile, Emerald felt a little better.

"We want you to look at this and tell us if you can make out the person in this feed." The officer, Officer Waller, told her that they needed her to tell what she saw, even if it was nothing at all, and then talk about what had happened over the weekend.

The feed started up and she could see the pretty little street. There were several cars going by, but nothing that she could recognize. But then a hand was there knocking on the door and she held her breath. As soon as the door opened, the man stepped into the view.

"It's him. It's Nolan." Firm hands settled on her shoulders, and she knew it was Jul. "It's him. I'd know that face anywhere. He was also the one that was at the school I was at. He came there to talk to me, but I think he was going to kill me."

"We think so as well. I'm glad that you're taking this very seriously. And that you could recognize him. That's very good." Officer Waller looked at her partner and he got up to leave. "I wanted to ask you about your relationship with Bruce. When did you first go out with him?"

"I never dated him at all. I was at the bar on Tenth with a friend, and we were having a good time when Nolan came up to the table and told us he was ready to go. I thought he was talking to my friend, but he reached for me." Emerald looked at Jul when his hands tightened on her shoulders. He let her go but didn't leave her. She looked back at the officer. "I explained to him that I had no idea who he was, but he insisted that he and I had gone there together. After the bouncer came to help him out of the place, I never gave him another thought. But he continued to act as if we were dating or more. And he's been stalking me."

"He came back." Emerald nodded. "When was this? Dates are important if you have them, but we can figure it out later if you don't."

"It was a week later. March fourteenth. I was with another friend. I wasn't drinking either time, mind you, but Shaffer was. But not much. A beer I think." She asked him what his name was. "Shaffer Carlee; it was his birthday. Anyway, Nolan came up to us and started screaming at Shaffer to get away from me, that I was his wife. I tried to step between them but was knocked back. Then when the bouncer came this time, Nolan turned to me and said we have unfinished business. I had no idea what he meant."

"What happened then?"

Emerald had thought about that night often. She hated that she'd stood by and didn't help Shaffer, but there had been so many people that shifting wasn't possible.

"He was at the car. Mine. He was standing there waiting on us. And he had a bat. He beat poor Shaffer so badly. He hit me too, but I couldn't help him. There were too many people there." The officer nodded, understanding. "I had two broken ribs and had been hit in the head. But Shaffer was nearly dead when the ambulance finally got there. I'm not sure...he won't let me see him. He said...Nolan threatened him, and he won't see me. Or let me see him."

Officer Waller told her they had talked to Shaffer and that he was afraid to help them. "But you've given us enough to go on for now. I'd like to talk to you about him coming to the school and the weekend. What can you tell me about those encounters?"

Emerald told her everything she could remember. Even about how the system in the school wasn't working, and that they'd had no way of warning the other two classes. Officer Waller made notes and asked her a lot of questions, and in the end, Emerald felt as if she'd done all she could. She and Jul went home to their new house. But there was a warning from Officer Waller that scared her badly.

"He's going to try and find you, Ms. Erickson. And when he does, he won't be stable about his actions. Bruce is a schizophrenic. He may even be a bit of a psychopath and psychotic." Emerald felt her wolf move along her skin. "He'll kill you if he gets the chance, and anyone that is with you. If you can…if I were you I'd try to find him first and end him."

"And what will happen to me if I do that?"

Officer Waller stood up and smiled as she moved closer to her. "If your wolf takes care of him, then there will be little to nothing left of him to be found. And who would believe you'd be capable of such a thing?"

As the officer moved out of the room, leaving her there with Jul, she turned to him.

"She said I should kill him." Jul said he agreed. "I'll need help. And a lot of it. Alone a wolf can't take care of a man like she's suggesting."

"Then you take your sisters. But kill him. For us." He moved out of the room with her, taking her hand. Emerald was back in the limo before what was just said to her sunk in. They thought she could do this. They thought she could actually kill a man in cold blood.

# Chapter 8

Nolan knew he'd messed up, and how badly. He'd killed the woman across the hall and he'd not taken the time to clean up after himself. Her screams and that fucking whistle had brought the entire floor out of their apartments, and he'd had to do some quick running to get away. Christ almighty, he was going to get caught because of an old bag. And all because he'd thought to go and finish up with Erickson.

Nolan was on the run now. He'd had to go back to his place, of course, to get his things, but now he was riding around in his car — his clunker, he called it — trying to figure out where he could go until this blew over. There was his apartment over the abandoned garage, but he was almost afraid to go there too. Things were going to cool down soon. He just had to lay low. But going there kind of scared him a little. To admit that he needed to use it meant he was really fucked.

There were plans in place for this kind of thing. Not as well laid out as they should have been, because he'd never considered getting caught. He was just that good. Anything he thought would happen to him would have been death by a cop, not this stupid thing with the old woman. But the old bitch had seen him breaking into Erickson's apartment, and she'd blown that fucking whistle.

First things first. Two things going to shit in the same day was not going to ruin everything. Nolan decided that he wasn't going to let it. So the fucking bitch was dead? Not his fault. How the hell was he supposed to know that the old bat would come out of her apartment like some vigilante? She should have let him know that she was going to blow that fucking whistle like she was and it might not have scared him so badly. He might have had time to think before he snapped her fucking neck. And in front of all them witnesses.

And the thing with Erickson's apartment was not his fault either. Not all of it anyway. He should have scoped the place out a little better and made sure he wasn't caught. But damn it, somebody had changed the locks from the last time he'd been there, and he'd had to resort to breaking in.

"Okay, calm down." He liked the sound of his voice. It wasn't that he was talking to himself, but he wasn't alone. Nolan needed to reassure himself, and this was just helping. "Go to the apartment and rest. That's what you need to do."

He drove there and pulled his car into the building. Nolan sat there for several moments, just a few, so that he could calm himself. It would do him little good to panic. Things would work out. He was a professional, and professionals did not freak the fuck out.

Gathering up his gear, he went to the apartment. He'd bought the building some time ago with the thoughts of bringing his victims here to play. But it was too hard to tie them up, load them in the car, and get them in the building. So he nixed that idea and set up the upper part as a place he could get away if he needed a few moments to himself. Then he'd decided that it was the perfect place for him to hide out. It was, of course, under a fake name.

Darrell Bolton had been his very first murder. Nolan smiled at the memory. He'd been seventeen and Darrell had been twenty. The two of them had been very good friends and had wanted to see what it felt like to cut into someone. Nolan supposed he was lucky to have gone first.

They were only supposed to cut to see how much blood there was. But as soon as he'd cut into Darrell's leg, he knew that it wasn't going to be enough, and cut through his belly to his intestine with a quick swipe of his blade. It had taken his friend nearly two days to bleed out in the tall grass behind his parent's house, but Nolan couldn't be where he was now if not for his help.

The place was just as he'd left it. There were dust cloths on the furniture, what little there was of it…a bed, a chair, and a microwave. The refrigerator was new, as was the freezer that he kept stocked all the time. Once he was here, he'd been thinking, he didn't want to take the chance of going out for a pizza. This was his place of cover, and going out for food would defeat the purpose behind that.

There was a television but no cable. He didn't think his company would give him free access to a second account, so he was without it here. Which, he supposed, was all right. He had a lot of movies on his computer that he'd downloaded, and figured he was set.

The bed was a problem. He'd kept thinking that he needed to get a bigger one, but the twin would have to do for now. Nolan knew that he was a big man; not fat, but he was tall. At six foot three, a twin just didn't cut it.

He made up the bed with the sheets he'd sealed in plastic and then lay down. He was tired because of the added stress, and knew that he'd think better if he had a nap. He was ready to close his eyes when his cell phone rang.

It was work. He wondered what the hell they might want. Nolan had done all the jobs, except the one with the dead woman's house. Instead of answering it, he let it go to voicemail. He was off and there was no way they were going to call him in this late.

The phone signaled that he had a message, and he smiled. Closing his eyes again, he let his mind drift over the events of the day. He had to have a better plan. Today was a major fuck up.

"First thing is that I have to finish those last two projects. Winter has to go, and so does Erickson. Both of them left me high and dry." He got up to get his notebook to make notes on the murder of the old broad, but couldn't find it. "I left it in the car. It's in the car. Don't panic."

But he was and he knew it. Going down to his car, he searched everywhere, even taking out the carpet in the trunk and floorboards. Nothing. It wasn't with him. He had to think again…his mind was spinning. If he lost that…well, worse if it fell into the wrong hands. He was so fucked.

Nolan got into his car and started for his place. It had to be there. He remembered taking it out of the floor and putting it on the duffle he was packing. There was something that made him turn around, something on the television, but he'd been too busy to focus too much. It had to be still on the table, and if it was, then he'd just go in, get it, and get the fuck out.

"Easy. It's going to be right there. Easy." He kept nodding to himself and saying it over and over. "Easy, easy, easy." But as he turned on his street, he knew that easy had just gone out the door with the trash. They knew where he had been living.

There were about twelve cruisers around his building. An ambulance had him hoping that someone was sick, but nothing was going to be that easy. Parking his car, he sat there watching things as they unraveled, and wondered if he should chance going to see. But when one of the cops came out, he was holding his notebook, wrapped in plastic. Nolan knew then that someone had placed him at Erickson's apartment, and now they were looking for him.

Nolan started his car and turned at the next street. He left his mind blank, knowing that if he thought about all the things in that notebook, all the notes he'd kept and pictures of the dead bitches, he was going to go into panic mode. And that would not help matters right now.

The drive back to his new place was done in a blur. Had he stopped at lights? Used his turning signal? Christ, he hoped so. Right now he did not need to be pulled over for anything. When he next became aware of his surroundings, he was sitting at his table and had a gun in his hand. He laid it gently on the table and tried to think if he'd been planning to end his life. He didn't think things were that bad, were they? Close, but not that bad yet.

"Now what?" There was no plan for this. Nothing. He'd fucked up so badly by leaving his book that he had no idea what to do now. Did he turn himself in? Did he leave the country? Could he?

Nolan went back to his bedroom and lay down. Panic mode was taking over, and he needed to calm down. Closing his eyes, he tried to think of anything other than what was happening to him right now. And his thoughts drifted to Erickson. He had no idea why, but he let them center on her.

The thoughts of killing her calmed him. Making her suffer as he was right now was a priority. As he began to drift off to sleep, he thought of all the ways he was going to hurt her. Cutting her wouldn't do. She needed to suffer. Smiling, he felt his mind calm, his body relax, and in no time, he was asleep. Erickson was going to make things right for him, even if she didn't know it yet.

~~~

Jul watched Em pace. She did that almost as much as he did. The security team that he'd hired was patrolling the property, and the gatehouse was now set up to not allow anyone but family in. And they were being very careful as well. He didn't want anything to happen to Em, not ever.

"Mr. Whitney, there's a gentleman at the gate. He says that he has an appointment with you. Mr. Colby Bass." He told Curtis to let him in. "He has his family with him as well. Shall I set up rooms for them?"

"Please. As well as...I was thinking that setting up a couple more rooms might be good. I know that my mom will be here today, as well as Blair and a couple of Ms. Em's family." Curtis nodded and walked away.

The staff had come with the house as the realtor had told them. And when Em had told them that she was a wolf, each of them nodded. He supposed working for a vampire had jaded them somewhat. But Curtis Mann had been the best thing that they could have gotten with the house.

He knew the house, the yards, and who was who in the area. The day they had moved in, he gave him a list of each person that worked there and what they did, as well as a list of what they might be. It had taken him ten minutes to figure out what the "h" was next to some of the names, and Em had laughed for another hour after telling him it was for "human." The rest had been easy in comparison.

Colby came into the house with his wife and children. They stood behind the lovely young woman who looked to be pregnant until Em came down the stairs and greeted them. She got down on the floor and spoke to them as if she'd known just what they needed to come out of hiding.

"Hello, my name is Em. Well, it's Emerald, but Jul calls me Em. You must be Jane and Austin. And you must be Darcy. Your family must like Jane Austen." The taller little boy nodded. "I bet you guys are hungry. I have had Curtis, the big man in the kitchen, fixing stuff; he's been working all day for you guys. I even had to have him tell me what ants on a log were."

"Celery with peanut butter and raisins." Em nodded and Jul watched the little girl move to stand beside her brother when he spoke. "We like peanut butter and banana sandwiches. They're the best."

"Are they?" Em stood up and put out her hand. "If you and your mom will come with me, we'll go and see if Curtis knows anything about those. I bet he doesn't. He's really smart, but I bet he's never eaten one of those before."

As they walked off, Jul looked up at Colby. The man was staring at him as if he knew something that he didn't. Which was more than likely true. The man was a wonder.

"You've a mate." Jul laughed and nodded. "A wolf too. Nice. If you open a winery business here, can we stay? I'd have to clear it with the alpha first, of course, but this is a really nice place."

"I happen to know him too. He's my future brother-in-law. He's married to Em's sister." Colby grinned. "And I have a house for you and your family to move into. I've taken the liberty of buying one for you that is close to the school where Em teaches. The kids are already enrolled."

"You didn't waste any time." Jul told him that he didn't have time to waste. "You don't. The label's production lines are on hold. They're just waiting on the new artwork. The crop coming in from France, the grapes are perfect. I've been talking to the foreman there, and he said that—"

"Wait. Business is top on my list, but not first." Colby stopped talking and smiled. "How are you? How is the family? Growing, it looks like."

"It is. We're going to have a baby soon, and we're excited about that. The school sounds good. If she teaches like she interacts with my children and wife, I think they'll love it as well." They moved to his office as Colby spoke. "I take it you're not pissed about me not telling you what we are?"

"She's that good. And she was excited to meet you. And no, I'm not pissed. Surprised, but not mad. They thought I knew what they were, all of them, because they could smell you on me. And that is something I wanted to talk to you about as well." Jul sat at his desk and tried to think the best way to say this. He smiled. Straight up, he supposed. "I want you to...I have a favor to ask of you. It's not business related, but I need help with the family. I'm clueless about all things that are paranormal."

"You mean every one you've had contact with, or just the wolves? I can smell panther on you, as well as vampire. More vamp than anything." He told Colby about Sloan and Rufus helping him out. "They're related to you as well?"

"Yes. Em's sister is mated to the vampire who converted her. One of the other brothers is a wolf and panther. I guess that doesn't happen often, but in this case it was a good thing. And then there's the tiger that works with Jade. Oh, and she works with wild animals. A few bears might be shifters too, but I'm not entirely sure." Colby started laughing. Then the longer he sat there, the harder he laughed. Jul just let him. He thought his life had taken on a sort of surreal aspect as well.

"When you go into the paranormal field, you really go into it." He laughed again before nodding. "I'll help you were I can. Mostly I can direct you to the right people to get answers, but I would suggest you simply ask your family. They'll love helping you out."

As they drifted into business, Jul told him about the appointment they had with Sapphire and Blair tonight. The family was coming for dinner, and he wanted them to meet them. Colby said that he had to contact Blair.

"I'm in his territory and there are laws. He could get pissy with me about it and fine us. I'm not...coming here on your plane didn't cost us anything, but my wife had to miss work. Money will be tight for a while."

"I'm going to give you a raise and…and there is a job for your wife if she wants it." Colby started to shake his head. "I want to do this, Colby. You've uprooted your family to come here for me. I need to do this."

"I'll talk to my wife. She might…she's not going to like that I said anything to you about it." He could understand that. Em had hated when he asked her about her car. He wanted to buy her a new one and she said hers still worked.

Blair was at the gate ten minutes later. They hadn't called him as yet, and Colby was nervous. It was Jul's fault; they'd gotten to talking about the production lines here in the States and completely forgot.

"I'm sorry, alpha." Colby dropped to the floor and spread out. His mate came from the kitchen, and she did the same. The children, Jul noticed, stayed by Em. "We should have called you before coming here, but it was urgent and I had forgotten. Please don't punish my wife."

"I'm not sure where you came from, but I'm not a hard ass." Em laughed and Blair tuned to her. "Not with nice people. You're not a nice person."

"You love me and you know it." Em walked to the couple and helped Dawn up off the floor. "What do you think Sapphire would say if she knew you had a breeding woman on the floor?"

"She'd knock him on his ass too." Sapphire breezed into the room handing the baby, a little guy, to Jul. "Hold him like you would something that if you dropped it, I'd kill you."

Jul looked at Blair. The man was laughing, and he shoved the baby at him, but of course, he didn't take him. This wasn't funny. He'd never held a kid in his life. Blair just told Jul to get used to holding him, and he tried, but the guy was very squirmy. But then the kid—he thought his name was Carter—looked at him and smiled.

*Gets you in the heart, doesn't it?* He looked at Em when she spoke to him. *I love that little guy, and he's so sweet.*

*You should know that I'm never changing diapers.* She laughed and he smiled. Cuddling the little boy into his arms, he felt him relax against him. *I could get used to this.*

Colby and Blair were shaking hands when Jul decided that he wanted a house full of kids. He had no idea how to deal with them, but having them around was going to be fun. As they all entered the office again to work, he held onto Carter until his mom said he was sleeping. Jul hated to let him go.

"I want you to know first off, I don't care for Whitney Wines, the name you asked us to work with." Jul wanted to tell her that was what he wanted, but she went on before he could. "It sounds cheap, like you should have a wino holding the bottle up. Whitney and Williams sounded sharp, old world. Your name alone on the label doesn't project the same feelings. And the wine is top rated. I really enjoyed it."

"Thank you, I think." She nodded and he frowned. "But I want people to know it's the same wine they've been buying, but a different label."

"It's not the same wine." He looked at Colby when he spoke. "It's not. We lost part of our grapes when the storm hit our vinery about six months ago. The stuff that we're producing, the bottles that I sent to Mr. and Mrs. Henson, are not what you labeled with Mr. Williams."

"We have what you're making now?" Colby nodded at Blair's question. "Then we're going to go with that. Not saying it's new. People may not want to branch out with that when they're used to a certain taste. I would suggest you have an open house and serve the wine. Also the new line of cheese you have. The crackers, I understand, are still in mock-up mode."

"There have been some problems with the way they're being produced. Baking them in the ovens to the crispness that we want is failing." Sapphire nodded at his explanation. "I've called in a few people, but they aren't giving me any help."

"Because you didn't call me." Thad walked in just as he started to explain that they kept telling him he was doing it correctly, that it was the oven. "The ovens are fine. It's the flour you're using. I'm going to send over the expert I have on my staff. She'll get you straightened out in no time."

"Why would you do that? Help me as your competition?" He looked around the room when no one answered him. "I know that my crackers are going to be packaged as an adult kind of thing, but you are still making them too."

"We're family." Jul didn't think that was a good enough answer, but the rest of them did, it seemed. "None of us are going to make any money if we are constantly worrying about stepping on each other's toes. I make a line of crackers that are shaped like frogs and sheep. They're for lunch boxes for children. The others, the ones for the adults, are round. Not because they're trying to be different, but because I was told they would look better when we marketed them."

"I only suggested you do that. I didn't say you had to." He looked at Sapphire as she continued. "Round was what we needed to fit in the containers. No one else makes round ones but those really expensive ones. Cracker sales were down on his line because they were buying another brand and putting them in the refillable containers. Since he made them round, sales have gone through the roof."

"How much?" Sapphire looked at Thad, who was grinning. He wasn't sure he wanted to know. When he told him, Jul sat down and stared at Sapphire. "You tell me what you have in mind and I'll do it. I want those kinds of numbers."

"Good. I have an idea in mind." As they worked around the label design and names, he noticed that everyone seemed to be relaxed and open. Blair, even being the alpha, treated everyone with respect, and didn't order anyone to take his idea as gospel. And when his mom came into the room, he had to hide his smile when she started in on Colby about not telling him what he was.

Jul realized in that second that this was his family, and he would do anything in the world to keep them safe and with him. At noon the rest of the gems came over, as well as their spouses, with the exception of Sloan and Rufus. Being vampires, even as old as they were, they needed to wait until the day was a little later into the evening.

Curtis announced lunch a few minutes later, and they all moved to the dining room. But with one look at Em, he knew that something was wrong. Going to her, he pulled her into his arms. She told him that she had lost her job at the school.

"Good." He looked at Blair and wanted to sock him in the nose. "We're expanding the school with the pack, and I was going to talk to you about running it. This will make it easier to convince you."

The entire lunch was centered on her new job and her hiring Dawn as her assistant. Everyone was thrilled. Even Jul thought it was the best idea. She'd be safe and with people who loved her as much as he did. And that, to him, was the best thing ever.

# Chapter 9

Nolan listened to the message twice before he decided that it was a scam. "Come in to the office to discuss your options" was too vague, too...too nothing. The company that he worked for would have called him before the cable company would have, and he also knew that his options were not up for another sixteen months. They wanted him there so they could question him.

He'd been thinking a lot about the book. His book. There was a great deal of incriminating information in it, but nothing they could tie to him. The writing in it was all printed in block letters. The pictures were printed on the printer he'd brought with him. Every time he'd sent one to his email address, he'd been careful to delete it. The same from his phone. There was nothing there either. Even if they got onto his computer, he'd taken all that stuff off it and had made sure that his history was erased daily.

Nolan knew that the book had been found in his apartment, but he thought he had a good case in claiming that it wasn't his. That someone had planted it. He was also counting on the fact that he was a good man, had a steady job, and he was well respected. Because, he thought with a smile, if you didn't respect him, then he simply killed you.

Having a plan worked out as to why he wasn't home was harder. He didn't have any family left. His mom had died some years ago. He had no idea where or even who his dad was. There were no sisters or brothers as far as he knew, and if he had any other family, it was news to him. So him using one of them as an excuse was out of the question.

There was his plan about being hurt. So far that one, to him anyway, had the most merit in being true. He'd been mugged, or better yet, shot. Eyeing the gun again, he wondered if the wound at his side was simply too old and he'd have to shoot himself all over again. Maybe he'd have someone else shoot him, but that brought up a whole new set of issues. They would talk. Or kill him outright.

Stabbing would work, but he had no knife, and he was actually more afraid of a knife than he was a gun. A person could hurt himself so quickly with a knife, with just a slip of it. It's why he always used his box knife when cutting someone to kill them. It was at a controlled depth, one that was deep enough to make them bleed, but not so much that he could be hurt if they got it from him. He had a thought that his logic was all wrong, but he was thinking about too many things to let that bother him.

After another hour of going back and forth, his phone ringing numerous times, Nolan decided on a bullet. He had to wipe it down, of course, make sure that the bullet had none of his prints on it, nor any of his DNA. He'd seen that somewhere on one of the cable shows. But that still left the problem that he had to have been somewhere so they'd not think he did it…he needed an alibi.

His phone. He would say he'd lost his phone. Brilliant, he thought to himself, and tried to think how to get rid of it. There were tracking things in it, he knew that much, and he was positive that once he reported it missing, someone somewhere would be able to track it.

He was living in the wrong sort of town, but he knew that if someone really started looking—and he was pretty sure they would for a murder or two—that they'd find his place. And as much as it was disposable, it would have enough evidence in it to show that he'd been there.

So now, where was he going to be robbed and shot? He'd been all over this town, so he had to know of at least one or two places to be mugged.

There was the warehouse downtown that had recently been converted to a homeless hang out. Bartholomew P. Winchester House of Rest, he remembered now. Stupid name. As if they had some sort of class, or something. He hadn't been assigned to go in and wire the place up with cable, but those that had said it was nice. Nicer than their own homes.

"Sure it was." He was liking the idea of going there. There would be enough of the bad element around that someone would be thought of as shooting him, and he'd be found pretty quick if the bullet was in a bad place. But first, he had business.

Erickson had to be dealt with. He wanted her dead for no other reason than he just did. Tomorrow he was going to get into the school and take care of her there. The place where she used to live, the one where he'd killed the old broad, was off limits to him, of course, so he had to go to the school. Maybe—and this was as far-fetched as him going to jail for his crimes—by the time he took care of Erickson, things would have blown over, and he'd save this plan for another time. By dinner he was confident that things would be worked out.

His phone rang again, and this time he thought about picking it up. Lucky for him he'd put a sticky note on it to ignore it. When a person heard a phone ringing, he'd come to realize, they just had to answer it.

By ten-thirty he was headed to bed. Looking out his small window, he saw some movement around the big parking lot, but knew there were all kinds of creepy people that only moved at this time. Vagrants mostly. Some prostitutes too. Not that he'd ever used one, but he knew where they hung out. But when someone knocked on the door to his hideaway, he nearly screamed.

"Mr. Bruce?" He didn't answer the call of his name, but moved closer to the door. "Mr. Nolan Bruce? I have a message for you."

He thought he heard the person laugh, but couldn't understand why he'd be laughing and waited. Finally the person said that they'd leave it on the step and he could pick it up at his convenience. Nolan waited almost an hour before he opened the door.

The envelope wasn't thick. And if it held anything other than a few sheets of paper in it, he couldn't for the life of him figure out what it might be. But the name printed on the front, in block letters as he'd used in his book, was what had him worried. It looked as if he might have written it himself.

Opening it was terrifying. If he did, was it like admitting something? He had no idea, but he stared at the thing for another hour before he even considered it. When he did open the thing up, his hands were shaking so hard he could hardly hold onto to it. Reading it was going to have to wait until he calmed a little.

By nearly two in the morning, he'd finally taken the letter to the living room and read it by flashlight. He'd turned off all the lights when he'd gone to his bedroom, and he didn't want whoever had left it for him to think he was home and, given that, cared about what was in the stupid thing. So he was trying to work it out when it became clear who had sent it.

"Hello Stupid." Nolan frowned at the greeting. Whoever had written to him was rude, and should have taken better care than to write such a thing. As he read on, however, he realized not only who had written the letter to him, but why.

"I want you to leave me alone. Actually, what I want is for you to go to hell, but since we both know that is where you're going to end up, we'll both just have to wait. But leaving me alone will let you live a little longer. Maybe.

"I have a family that will tear you to shreds. Not that I didn't have them before, but when you went to my school and fucked with me there, you brought all of them to your doorstep. And trust me when I tell you, you've barked up the wrong tree with that one. They're wolves."

Nolan had to laugh. If Erickson thought her family was wolves, he wondered why she would bother telling him to be afraid. Wolves indeed. He was...Nolan tried to think of something that was more of a predator than a wolf, and came up with a hawk. They could fly and swoop down and kill their prey, while the stupid dog that she'd compared her family to could only walk in the woods. His bird of prey was much fiercer. He continued with the letter.

"If for some reason you don't have the brains to listen up, you can find me at the warehouse downtown. It's called Winchester House, if you need to ask. Most people know where that is." He had to grin. Just where he was headed anyway. Two birds—or in her case, a bitch dead and an accident for him—in one place. "I'll be there tomorrow night at seven. No cops will be there, even though there should be." Her name was at the bottom.

Nolan went to his bed again. Rest would come easy now; things were falling into place and he'd have it all taken care of by the day after tomorrow. He was almost too excited to sleep. It was as if he knew he was going to watch blood pour from the bitch, and he was going to get to have the climax of his life.

~~~

Emerald wasn't thrilled with the plan. It was a good one, but not that good. So many things could go wrong. She was pretty sure that she'd thought of nearly all of them and had tried to work out a plan to counteract them, but there was going to be one thing, just one, that she'd not thought of that was going to fuck it up.

She looked up when Jul said her name. "You're going to have a head explosion if you keep thinking that hard."

"I'm worried about so many things that could go wrong." He came into the sitting room that was part of their suite and sat beside her on the couch. "He could not show, for one thing."

"I don't think that's going to happen. He, for some reason, isn't going to give up the chance to see you once more." That, too, frightened her a little. He was going to see her again. And there would be people around...mostly her family, but there would be others, and one of them could get hurt. "I'd do just about anything to see you if I didn't already have you here all the time. Bruce is going to be the same way."

Emerald turned so that she was sitting over his lap facing him. "You mean me or my body? I'm pretty sure you've seen every inch of me. For that matter, I think you've tasted me too."

"I have. But I can't seem to get enough of you." Jul unbuttoned her blouse and moved it down her shoulder. "The way you taste when you're aroused. The scent you give off when I touch you."

She let him pull her blouse off and felt his cock thicken beneath her. When he rocked upward, she rode him while he nipped at her breasts still cupped in her bra. Wrapping her hands around his shoulders, she moaned when he unclasped the front snap and freed her breasts. He wasted no time in pulling her right nipple into his mouth and suckling it as he pulled and tugged on the other. Her ride across him was getting more desperate, and she wanted him naked.

"Take off your pants." He moaned at her command. "Please, I want to ride you this way. Feel you inside of me."

He moved her off him and opened his pants. His cock was thick with need and leaking from the tip. Leaning over him, she licked her tongue over the pearly juices, and then took him into her mouth. All thoughts of riding him were gone now that she had him in her mouth.

She'd tasted him before, had him fuck her mouth while he laid out before her. But this time she moved to kneel between his legs as soon as she got his pants completely off. Cupping his balls in her hands, she marveled at their weight and took one of them into her mouth. He cried out and she thought she'd hurt him.

"More." His breathless voice made her want to have more of him, and she took him back into her mouth as she fisted him. Emerald loved his taste here, the way they tightened in her mouth, and she was enjoying that he was at her mercy.

When she licked up his shaft and took him into her mouth, he rolled his hips upward and she felt him at the back of her throat. Swallowing around him had him sliding past the tightness of her throat, and she no longer felt like she was going to strangle. When his fingers curled into her hair, she thought he was going to pull her way, but he pushed her down over him harder.

His balls were tight now, so close to his body that she could fit both of them into her hand while she let him fuck her mouth. Her pussy was so needy that she slid her hand down her pants and into her heat. She nearly cried out when she brushed against her clit. But Jul pulled her up before she could explore more.

"Bed." She was so close to coming that she had no idea what he wanted her to do. When he picked her up and carried her to the bed, she cried out when he dropped her onto it. "I want you to spread out. I'm going to eat you while you suck my cock. Then if I can, if you don't kill me first, I'm going to fuck you hard enough that you scream."

Spreading her legs for him, she watched him stare. Emerald was amazed at how wanton she felt when she was with him. The thought of him eating her pussy was making her wet, but when he got onto the bed with his cock at her mouth, she nearly came the moment he licked her pussy.

Nothing would have prepared her for them having sex this way. He ate at her while fucking her mouth over and over until she screamed through a climax. Still he ate, licking her and sucking on her clit until she was sure she was going to die from it. When he rolled off her, his cock still wet from her mouth, she wanted to ride him again, but he moved before she could.

Jul tossed her over onto her belly and then lifted her ass up. He buried his cock into her so quickly that she came quick and hard. When he leaned over her, taking her like a wolf would a mate, she lowered her head and let him pound into her. Christ, she wanted him to be a wolf so she could feel him take her wolf like he was right now. When he paused, stopped moving over her, she felt his teeth graze her shoulder.

"If I bite you, draw blood, what happens to me?" She felt his teeth nip at her again, and she nearly came. "If I bite you, what happens?"

"I come. Harder than ever before." He bit her harder, and she had to breathe through the sudden need for him to do it before she could answer him. "You'll heal faster than before. Be stronger too. Not as much as I, but...please, bite me."

"I'm going to." Him licking her shoulder had her sliding her fingers to her pussy when he started to move again. "I want you to convert me. I want to be your mate in all ways. Can we do that?"

Yes, her mind screamed, but it wasn't that simple. "I have to get permission from Blair. You'll…Christ, just bite me, please?"

His teeth sank into her hard. The moment he broke the skin, she felt her climax take her. Grabbing his arm that was nearest to her, she bit him as well, let her wolf mark him while she tasted his hot spiked blood. His cum filled her with his heat and seed, and she came again. Emerald felt as if he was marking her the way her kind did, and when he tore at her shoulder, she came again. This time her wolf made her own pleasure known. The howl that spilled from her was primal and loud. Then she bit him again and heard bones break. His screams were cut off when he fell forward over her.

He was out for no longer than ten minutes. In the whole time she never left him, only to go and get a wet cloth to put over his bloodied face. At first she thought it was his, but after cleaning him up, she figured out it was hers. He'd marked her, and that was all it was. As soon as he opened his eyes, she burst into tears.

"I'm fine, love. Seriously, I don't hurt at all." She crawled in to be next to him and held him tightly against her, while he told her over and over how great he felt. She noticed that his wrist was already healing.

"You've a great deal of me inside of you." She showed him how she'd shattered his wrist and that it was healing. "But this is nothing compared to what it will be like when I change you. I have to really hurt you. I mean, tear into you like I'm going to kill you."

"I trust you." But she didn't trust herself and told him that. "But you will do it? You're going to change me into a wolf? For us?"

"I don't know if I can." He held her but said nothing. "I have to bite into you hard enough to bring you to near death. That way your body can heal it and you while it makes the change. I've only seen it done once before, and that was because the person was nearly dead anyway. Lucky for her, her mate was strong enough not to stop the process when everyone feared that he'd killed her."

"You won't let me die." She was glad that he had so much confidence in her, because she certainly didn't. "I talked to Dawn at dinner, along with Thad and Quentin. Both of them said that they'd been changed or they would have died. Dawn said that Colby changed her because she'd become his mate. She had the most information on it."

"Blair might not let me." She knew that he would say she could, but she wasn't a hundred percent positive. "And then because of you wanting to do this without it being an emergency, we have to do it in front of the pack. When Ruby changed Josh, there wasn't permission given and they had to be punished. I'm not sure how much of a punishment it's been for them. They seem to enjoy being in charge of their pack."

He rolled her to her back and looked at her. "I love you. More than I ever thought I could love a single person. I want to be with you, like you, and a part of you. If Blair says no, whatever the punishment is, I'll gladly do it to be a wolf like you. I love you very much."

As he moved over her and then back, she wondered how hard it would really be if Blair said no. But when Jul took her hand and then slipped a ring over her knuckle, her mind went completely blank. He held it in a way that she couldn't see what it looked like, not even the band.

"It's a ring." He laughed and nodded. "You didn't have to give me a ring. I mean, whatever it looks like, I'm sure that it's very lovely, but I don't have to have a ring. Can I see it?"

He moved his fingers out of the way and then turned it so that the stone was on the top. Emerald looked at it for several seconds before she looked up at him.

"I wanted to give you all the diamonds in the world, but that seemed mundane after seeing your sister's rings. And then when I saw that each of them had a ring that was basically their name, I had to be different. You know, be the best." He laughed when she nodded. "I've rendered you speechless, haven't I?"

"I don't know what to say." She didn't either. The ring...well to call it a ring was like calling this place a shack. "Did you design this?"

"My mom helped, but yes, I did. It was easy compared to working up the courage to ask you to be my wife."

She sat up, unmindful of her nudity, and stared at the setting. "There is one of each of us here, isn't there?"

The base stone was an emerald, a round cut one that sparkled around the room. There was a small sapphire, diamond, jade, opal, then a ruby. They repeated themselves twice as they surrounded the stone. The band, a platinum one that was as wide as her first knuckle, balanced out the ring and made it look dainty rather than heavy and crass. And on the band were wolves, each of them chasing the other all the way around. Jul told her to look on the inside.

"'Forever true is my love for you.'" Then there were their initials as well as the year. Emerald looked up at him again.

"I love you." He nodded and said he loved her as well. "I will convert you. As soon as we get this thing with the bastard completed, I'll do it. With or without Blair's permission."

"Good. I love you very much too." He pulled her into his arms and held her while he continued. "This plan tomorrow. I need to ask you a few questions. Like what the hell are we supposed to do if he brings a gun?"

She explained to him that bullets would hurt like hell, but unless it was silver, they could survive it. "But not to the head or heart. We will die from that like any human."

They spent most of the night talking about the plan. Then when he seemed satisfied, they talked about his business and her new job. By the time the sun was coming up, Jul had fallen asleep and she lay there looking at him. Sapphire touched her mind, and she asked her to come to the kitchen.

*I'm lonely.* Emerald dressed as she kept staring at the ring and went to keep her sister company. It was going to be a long day.

# Chapter 10

Nolan arrived early. He wasn't stupid enough to think that there wouldn't be some sort of backup plan. This thing with Erickson was going to be fun and all, but shit, he knew it wasn't going to be that easy. So when he arrived at the homeless place at two, he was surprised to find several delivery trucks backed up to it, as well as about fifty people unloading them.

From the amount of food coming out of those trucks, he wondered what the hell else was going on inside the place. There had to be enough food going in there to feed a thousand people. Or more. His belly rumbled as he watched. The thought of going in there and taking a few things to fill the void was making him slightly ill.

His food had run out the day before yesterday. And while he had some money, the one time he'd gone out to get some supplies he'd almost been caught. Whoever the broad was that had started screaming it was him was not going to be telling anyone who he was for a long while, if ever. He'd hit her pretty hard with his car when she'd come out of the store looking for him again. Christ, Nolan thought it would have blown over by now.

He was hoping that after today, when Erickson was dead, things would get back to normal. Nolan was making plans to go back to working with the cable company again, and cleaning out his apartment of all the shit that the cops might have done to it. And getting him another notebook. He really would miss his other one, but it wasn't like he could ask for it back. That would fuck up his entire plan.

By three he was thinking that he was going to leave and come back. There was nothing going on here but a bunch of trucks coming in and going out, and some homeless shits getting a few meals.

The guy who seemed to be in charge was having things set up outside when he got out of his car to walk to the convenience store at the corner. It looked like they were getting ready for a concert or something, and he wondered who the headliners might be. Still, by the time he'd returned to his car with three of them roller dogs and a bag of chips with a six pack of beer, things didn't look like Erickson and her family of wolves were even going to show up.

Nolan must have fallen asleep at some point. When he woke up and looked around, things were a great deal different than they'd been when he'd parked there. The chairs were set up in lines, and this time he knew it wasn't a concert but a wedding. The big bunches of flowers and the trellis were his first hint, and the band setting up told him the rest. Who the hell got married in a homeless shelter?

There were people already seated in a few of the seats. He looked at the clock on his phone and was surprised to see it was just going on five-thirty. If he was meeting Erickson here at seven, then the wedding was going to take place about the same time. Great, he'd have a distraction when he left her dead body lying there.

At ten minutes to six, a long limo pulled up. Nolan sat up higher in his seat and watched the couple getting out. He had no idea who they were, or again what the hell they were doing here, but he watched them enter the warehouse. Twice more limos came and left people before he finally got out of his car to go and have himself a look at what the hell might be going on.

The place was done up like some sort of Christmas pageant. He'd never been to one, but he'd seen pictures of them. While he was standing there looking around, he was bumped from behind by another couple as they made their way inside. That was when he noticed the Christmas tree and all the gifts under it.

"It's July," the woman behind him laughed. "What the hell is going on? Christmas is not for another six months."

"It's a charity ball. We're raising money to help children and families celebrate the holiday. We're hoping to have enough money so that each family has a lovely meal and presents for everyone in the family. Last year we surpassed our goal by nearly ten grand. I think we'll make more than that this year." She looked around. "I think this was a grand place to have it this year, don't you?"

Nolan didn't bother answering her. She was nuts. Who the hell wanted to help the homeless out anyway? And to raise money for them was just dumb. They'd be spending it on beer and drugs before even one dime went to getting a gift.

He'd been in the system when he'd been a kid. Some woman would come along and ask his mom what size clothes he wore and what one gift he wanted more than anything. His mother had been the dumbest thing on earth. She'd told the woman that all she wanted for her son was a good coat.

"A coat." He looked around when he realized that he'd spoken out loud. She'd told the social worker that he'd not needed anything but a warm coat, and that was all he'd gotten, except a few other things that were just as useless; a pair of boots that were too small, a backpack filled with school supplies, and underwear. Who the hell got a kid underwear for Christmas?

At a quarter till seven, after sampling everything on the buffet line, he went outside again. The bride and groom weren't anywhere he could see them, and even though a few more of the seats were filled with fat asses, it didn't look as if that part of tonight's shindig was going to happen any time soon.

He was back at his car, leaning on it this time, when he saw her. She was dressed in a pair of jeans and a shirt. There were two other women with her that were dressed the same, but he had no idea where they were going. As they headed around the building, he moved behind them. He had his belly full now, and things were looking up.

As he rounded the corner, there was a man sitting in a chair. It was one of the wedding chairs, and he stood up when he saw him. The man didn't move, but Nolan watched him carefully.

"You must be Nolan Bruce." Before he could think this was a trap, Nolan nodded. "Good. I've been waiting for you to come around. The woman are waiting for you to get here before they come out. But you should know that…well, you're not leaving here. I just thought you'd like to know that before they get out here."

"Come out of where? And what the fuck are you doing here anyway?" The man didn't answer but sat back down. "What the hell is going on? I was supposed to meet Erickson here. And as for me not leaving here? I think you got it all wrong, buddy. I'm going out the same way I came in. On my own two feet."

"No, you're not."

Nolan was getting pissed. He had things to do. Well, not really, but this wasn't what he had planned. When the man laughed, he looked at him again.

"What the hell is going on? I want answers, not you sitting there giggling like some school girl on her first date." The man stood again and Nolan realized how tall he was. At least five or six inches taller than him. "Who are you? And why should I believe a single word coming out of that puss of yours?"

"My name is Blair Henson. These men," Nolan turned when he pointed behind him, "…are Thad Galloway, Quentin Witt, Sloan Crane, and Josh Ewing. Oh, and that man coming from over there is Jul Whitney. We're all married, or in Jul's case, about to be married, to the Gems. You ever heard of them? They're something special, our gems."

"I'm here to see—" The man cut him off. And that was one of Nolan's most hated crimes as far as he was concerned, cutting someone off when they were talking.

"So you said, you're here to meet with Erickson." Henson sat down, and the men, who Nolan just noticed had been carrying their own chairs, joined him. They were all facing him and looking as relaxed as men at a bar looked when they'd had a few. When Henson nodded in that direction, Nolan turned. "They're here now. And as they all were Erickson's at one time, I think you should know that they're sisters. All six of them."

"Fuck." The six big dogs that were standing there looked like something out of a nightmare. His nightmare. As they started toward him, he heard one of the men tell him not to run. He started to ask why when he answered him.

"They like to run down their prey. The first time I met Emerald I'd been told not to run. But I did and...well, I'm pretty sure your encounter with her won't be nearly as enjoyable as mine was." He laughed again. "She said something to me today about it being the best way to kill someone. Just to run them down and tear out their throat. I'm betting you don't last that long, but it will be fun to watch you die."

"What the hell are you talking about?" The man didn't answer him, and Nolan turned then. "I don't know what the fuck is going on, but you call them dogs off right now. This isn't the way I had it planned out. And I like a plan."

"Wolves." He looked at the man who'd sat down next to Henson. "They're not dogs, but wolves. They're our wives. You should also know that they hate being called dogs. Bitches is okay, but not dogs. Brings their pissyness out, and that's not ever pretty."

"You're one sick motherfucker. I want you to call them off. I don't give a shit what they are, but you bring out that Erickson bitch, the one called Emerald, and we'll have our talk." He turned back to see that the wolves had cut the distance between him and them in half. And the closer they got to him, the bigger they got. Now he could see that they were indeed wolves. "What the hell are they doing loose anyway? Somebody should call the dog pound and have them gathered up. They might cause some harm to some kid or something."

He took a step back and stopped when one of them growled. Teeth shone brightly in the moonlight, and he nearly took another step back when Henson told him to stop. Nolan felt the hair on his arms dance when one of them, the closest one to him, snarled at him. Sweat poured down his back as it swiped its paw at his leg.

"You said you wanted to talk to Erickson. Well, here they are. All of them. I do believe that Em told you she was bringing her family and that they were indeed wolves." Nolan turned and looked at the man…Jul, he'd been told his name was. "She and her sisters have decided that there is just too much at stake to let you go to trial. One of them suggested that you'd plead insanity and get out in a few years. That wasn't acceptable to them. So, they're going to take care of you right now. And if you think that the police are going to give a shit that they're going to kill you, think again. They were told by one of them that this is the only way to handle it. Killing you is the best way to rid this world of scum like you."

"I'm not going to trial, and they sure as shit aren't going to be taking care of me. If any of them come close to me, I'm going to kill them." The man on the end laughed. "You think this is funny there, boy? What if I told you that after I finish with your wives, I'm going to kill you too?" He reached for his gun and couldn't find it. The man laughed again.

"I've already taken it from you." The gun dropped in front of the man. "And if you manage to get out of this, which is highly doubtful, you should learn to bring silver to a wolf fight. Those bullets wouldn't have hurt any of them. Pissed them off, but not hurt them overly much."

When a hot breath fell over his fingers, Nolan jerked his hand back and turned. The wolves were standing close enough that he could have touched them. The first one growled low and snarled at him. Nolan took a step back, then another as they advanced toward him in a line.

The softly spoken "Run" had him turning and taking off. He had gone perhaps ten feet when he remembered he'd been told not to. When something hit him in the back, he fell forward. The pain in his leg, the feeling that it was being bitten, had him looking back. Nolan screamed. They were all over him in seconds.

The pain was incredible. He knew they were playing with him, knew that for some reason they weren't killing him right away. But when they all backed off save one, he looked up at her with blood tinged eyes. Everything in his body hurt, and he was pretty sure that he was bleeding to death. In seconds the wolf was gone, and Erickson was kneeling in front of him.

"I wanted you to see what happens to fucking idiots that mess with my family." He grinned at her and felt his mouth not working right. He did speak...slurred, but he spoke to her.

"I'm coming to get you, bitch. And when I do, this is going to look like nothing." He felt the hands wrap around his head. It reminded him of the hat he'd gotten for that Christmas. "You're going to wish for death."

"No. You'll be dead in seconds." He felt the grip tighten around his head and knew that whoever it was, they were going to snap his neck. The last thing he saw before the person twisted him was Erickson blowing him a kiss.

~~~

Ten minutes. Jul had ten minutes to straighten up or he was going to be late. When someone knocked on the door for the tenth time, he turned to scream at them to leave him the fuck alone for five minutes. But the door opened and his mom was standing there.

"You're going to be fine." He nodded. Not because he believed her but because she did. "Em is a lovely young woman and will make you happier than you've ever been."

She took his tie from him and put it around his neck as he thought of what he was about to do. "She still mad at me about this?"

"I don't think so. I think she's still trying to decide which of her sisters she wants to murder more. She's under the impression that someone, one of them, should have told her what you were doing." He nodded as she finished tying his tie. "And the way that her grandmother is fussing with her dress, I'd say she's on the list too."

"Thank you for helping me out with it. I would never have thought of using yours." She nodded as she fussed with his handkerchief. "How did you know it would fit her?"

"Annabelle told me." His mom stepped back and looked him over. "You look as handsome as your father right now. I'm surprised all the time by how much you favor him."

"I miss him too." She nodded and he pulled her into his arms to hold her. "Mom, I love Em with all my heart. I don't know what I'd do without her."

"She loves you too. Very much." She looked up at him. "What does she think about the little girl?"

Em had come to him about the child. She'd told him the entire story about how the little girl's brother, one of her students who had been murdered by his parents. Em had also told him how Sloan had taken care of his parents' bodies after he'd killed them both. No one would ever find them, and he'd made the way clear for the little girl, the only survivor of the horrific night, to be adopted. She'd told him that she was going to help with that. He'd told her they should be her parents.

"I think she's going to make a great mom." She smiled at him. "And you an awesome grandmother. You're going to have her spoiled before she's settled, aren't you?"

"And why not?" He knew for a fact that her room had already been painted in her favorite color of yellow, and that her closet was full. Jul held his mom as he thought of the little girl, Noelle Shoot.

"Opal took away her memories of that night." He felt his mom nod. "She couldn't take away all the memories because she wanted her to remember her brother. But she was able to change them around so that there was a great deal less trauma. There will still be problems, we think, but nothing like they might have been for her. She's going to get the best of everything from now on."

"Of course she will. And with a family like this one, she'll be loved more than any other child could be. But what of her memories of her parents? Does she have any good memories of them?" He'd asked Opal the same thing, and she'd told him none. He told his mom that.

"I think that had Sloan not killed them, I would have. To have something so precious and treat it so horrifically…. They should have gotten the worst kind of treatment." Sloan had told him that he'd killed them both, but he'd never said how. Blair had assured him that he didn't want to know either. He had a feeling that Sloan had told him, and it had bothered the big alpha a great deal.

The knock at the door had them both turning to it. It was time. He was going to be married to the most wonderful woman in the world, and he couldn't wait. Before he and his mom left the room, she asked him for one more second.

"I loved your father. Miss him every day of my life. But having you as my son has eased my pain a great deal and made living easier. I could not have asked for a better person than you in my life." He kissed her on the cheek, and she pulled back, obviously not finished. "But if you hurt her in any way, make her cry for any reason whatsoever, I will bring an Armageddon down on you so quickly, you won't have time to hide."

She walked out of the room in front of him. Jul looked up at Allen, who was going to serve as father to the bride. He was laughing so hard that he had to hold onto the wall next to him. He was still laughing when they walked to the front of the podium set up just for this event. The people at the charity ball were serving as their guests tonight, as well as witnesses. Jul looked at the men who had stood up with him, and felt the feeling of family wash over him again.

Sapphire had set up everything for him. And when he'd told her what he wanted, she'd jumped on the wagon and taken over. The only time he'd had to answer anything about what she'd planned was the pastor. The rest she'd done on her own. So when she came out of the building in front of him, he had to smile. He should have known.

Her dress was the blue of her name. The stars above them made it sparkle and seemingly dance around her. When she was joined with Blair at the end of the line, he looked up to see Diamond come out.

Her dress was no less brilliant and shone like a bright diamond around her. Her belly, full of hers and Thad's child, seemed to be highlighted by the candles around the guests. Jul smiled when she blew him a kiss. He might have to hug her again later, now that he knew what it meant to her husband.

The next gem to come down the line was Jade. The green of her dress was as beautiful as the grasses of Ireland. The way it moved around her, shimmering no less than the other two, reminded him of the pull and flow of the rivers he'd walked along while there a few years ago. She wore it long, unlike her two older sisters who had worn shorter dresses.

Next came Opal, and her beauty surpassed that of the gem she was named for. Her dress was opaque in color with brilliant stripes of white and pale blues. When she winked at him, he had to laugh and felt that whatever came next was going to be epic.

Ruby was a woman who danced to her own drum. The red of the dress was nearly blinding. She wore it like it had been born to her as skin. Unlike her sister's dresses that flowed around them, Ruby's shimmered down her body and in a fall of red beads, and in her hair was a long streak of blood red. Jul could only shake his head at her. She giggled when she stood with him, and smiled when he winked back. Jul knew that for so long as he lived, this family, his family, was never going to be boring.

There was a long pause before his bride came out. He was worried for a moment until the wedding march was played. As the crowd stood up, Jul held his breath. He'd not seen her since she'd left him after Blair had killed Nolan. But this was not the time to think about what had transpired before this.

Jul wasn't prepared for her beauty. He knew she was, beautiful in all ways, but to see her now, with his mother's wedding dress on, he had to blink twice to assure himself that she was really coming toward him. But as she got closer to him, he started to chuckle. Then he laughed until he could hardly stand any longer. Sapphire had made everything perfect.

The dress fit her like it had been made especially for her. The train of the dress, long and lovely, was what had him laughing. The children, all two dozen of them, were dressed in the colors of the bride's maids that had preceded them. Two of them were even dressed in white. The streak of red in the hair of the two children dressed in red had him laughing harder. But it was Allen that had him nearly fall over. He was dressed in a white suit that looked like he'd stood back and let someone throw paints at him, all the colors of the gems that he loved so much.

When Em was handed off to him from Allen, he leaned in and whispered in his ear. "She wanted you to remember this day for the rest of your life."

He nodded. There would be no way he'd forget it, not with Em at his side. Turning to the pastor, he noticed that he too was having a good time. And when he asked if they were ready, Em said she needed just a moment.

"Today is my wedding day and without all of you, it would not have been this lovely. Thank you." She looked at him then. "With all my heart, I love you. All my life, I give to you. All my family is yours as well. My sisters and I have…we decided that since you are the last gem to be married into this family, we wanted to make this special for you as well. With all the other men in this family — our gems to us — we decided that nothing would be complete without you. We want to tell you how much we love and appreciate you for being a part of us."

Jul kissed her on the mouth, and she knelt down on her knee. "Honey, it's a little late to propose to me now. We're here to get married."

"Hush." She looked around at her family, then at him, before continuing. "I take you as my mate. I love you with my heart. I surrender myself to you. And I…and I…." She looked at Blair.

"And I give to you all that I am in any form, forever." She nodded and repeated what Blair had said. Then he leaned into him and whispered for him to kneel as well. "Say what's in your heart to her."

Nothing but how much he loved her came to mind. "I take you as my mate, and I will love you with all my heart. I surrender all that I have, all that I will ever have, to you forever. And I will love you in any form you take." Jul glanced at Blair before looking at Em again. "I will be your mate in all ways, love you forever, and I will never love you more than I do at this moment."

When they were both standing again, he looked at the pastor. He was wiping at his cheeks as he held his book in front of him. When he nodded that he was going to be fine, he started the ceremony that would bind them legally. But as far as Jul was concerned, they were already man and wife.

# Chapter 11

"These are the designs that we came up with. There are nine here for you to look over, and then we can work the name of your company in it easily enough." Sapphire handed him several sheets of photographic paper, and he glanced at them as she continued. "These are in black and white. I don't think you should go this route because you need something that makes people pause before moving to the next group of wines. Also, we've set up some—"

He raised his hand, and she stopped talking. "I'm slightly...majorly overwhelmed. Please. Just...I need a second here. It's too much too fast."

Jul leaned back in his chair and closed his eyes. He had been here with them for over three hours, and it had been nonstop. Not that he wasn't pleased with the amount of work they'd been able to get accomplished, but his mind wasn't up for it just yet.

"Are you worried about tonight?" He opened his eyes and looked at Blair. Sapphire was no longer in the room, and her assistants were gone too. "Things will go well. I have all the confidence in the world in you both."

"She's terrified." Blair nodded, and Jul sat up in his chair. "I think she's told me more than a dozen times a day of the things that could go wrong. How I might die, and that if she kills me she's asked for you to kill her as well."

"I won't do that. I told you that." Jul nodded. He knew that Blair would do the right thing, but damn it, he was afraid as well. "What's bothering you mostly about this? I mean, besides the possibility that you may die."

"She might not be able to do this. Not convert me, but live. I don't think she'll live if something goes wrong." Jul looked out the window. "I think she's more depressed now than when I first met her. I'm worried for her health too. Did you know that she's not eating all that much? Not since our wedding."

"I've had Sapphire and the other gems talk to her, but she keeps telling them she's fine. Today Opal and Jade are taking her shopping for the babies, and later tonight the rest of them are meeting her here to get ready. I think that she'll be with someone all day." Blair laughed and Jul looked at him. "We bombarded you on purpose."

Jul nodded. "I figured as much. To be honest with you, I'm less worried about me and this conversion than I am her at the moment. I know that things could go wrong. Hell, leaving this office today could get me killed. But she worries me. She's lost weight, rarely gets out of the house, and just last night she asked me about some of her things we'd been able to save from her apartment. I had to make a list of who got what. Scared the shit out of me."

The door to his office opened, and he turned to see Annabelle and Allen there. The two of them looked ready to do battle, and Jul stood up. He had no idea what he could do to help a pack of wolves, but he was ready. Annabelle sat down and told Allen to behave. Then she looked at him.

"I usually don't butt in...." She glared at Blair when he burst out laughing. "I will have you know that I do not butt into your affairs unless they might be harmful to you. But for now, I'm talking to this nice young man. You, my fine sir, can leave us."

Blair kissed Annabelle on the cheek and left them. Jul wasn't sure he wanted to be left alone with her, but when Allen handed him a tumbler of bourbon, he looked at his watch. It was just past eleven.

"You'll need it." He sipped the drink and set it down. If he needed it he wanted to be ready, not drunk before they began. "We want to help you shake up that gem of yours. She's not going to make it tonight if you don't heed what we're saying to you."

"You need to piss her off." He looked at Annabelle, then at Allen when she spoke. "I mean, really piss her off. Not to the point where she attacks you, but that she's upset."

"I can't do that. She's a wolf for one thing, and I'm not. Secondly, she's barely functioning right now. I doubt if I could get her just a little upset." Annabelle nodded. "I don't understand. How do you think that will help her?"

"If she's angry, she'll be able to make this work." Annabelle stood up to pace. "When Emerald was a little girl, there was a child down the street from us that would torment her daily. I mean to the point where she was in tears from it. All the girls offered her advice. Told her to punch the girl in the nose and be done with it. I'm betting you can tell which one said that."

"Jade." Annabelle nodded and grinned. "And what happened to the girl when she punched her? Did she stop?"

"Emerald didn't hit her. She ignored all their advice. And no matter how many times I had to hold her, she did nothing to her. Then one day Emerald came home with a bloodied lip and her dress torn. And since that day she and the little girl have been the best of friends." Annabelle sat down and Jul looked at Allen for an explanation. He only shrugged.

"She hit her anyway?" Annabelle shook her head. "You do that well, by the way. Lead someone up to the story ending then let them hang. What happened?"

"Thank you. There was another bully on the street. This one much bigger than the first girl, and by far larger than Emerald. That day the bully, a young man that has since been incarcerated several times, had the little girl down on the ground and was beating her with his fists. Emerald knocked him on his bottom. I mean, literally on his bottom. And every time he got up, she'd put him back there. I'm told it was a sight to behold."

Jul didn't understand. "You mean it was okay for this girl bully to beat up on her, but she didn't want her bully to be bullied? Why not? And if you tell me that you had something to do with this, I'm never going to trust you again."

"She needed something to bring her out of her shell." Jul watched her closely, waiting for Annabelle to tell him she was kidding. But she spoke again before he could tell her she was full of shit. "The bully wasn't my doing, Jul.

But I thank you for thinking me so wonderfully calculating. No, the female bully wasn't really hurting her physically. Teasing her, yes. Making fun of her, assuredly, but she never hit her. Emerald got mad when someone bigger was hurting a person who wasn't their peer. Wasn't in their weight class."

Jul thought about what she was saying. Emerald stepped up to the plate when the little girl was being hurt. It didn't matter to her that the child had been mean to her, it was the fact that she was being hurt now. And badly. But he had no idea what this had to do with him and tonight.

"She thinks that she's going to kill you when she does this." Jul nodded at Allen. "Tell her you believe that she will."

"I can't do that." Allen nodded. "I can't. She's already terrified that she'll kill me. And telling her that she will would...."

Jul thought about it again. Christ. She'd do it to prove him wrong. Or at least, that's what he thought Allen was saying to him. But what if it just tore down her confidence altogether? Then where would he be?

"You sly old devil you." Allen bowed before him. Of course, the man would take that as a compliment. "And if this doesn't work? What if she really does kill me?"

"She won't. And if it looks like you might not make it, Sloan and Blair will be right there with you." Jul nodded, liking this plan more and more as he thought about it. "She's extremely stubborn, in the event you didn't know that."

"I know that." He grinned. "And you might be right. She might just make this work. And if she does, then I'll be indebted to you both for the rest of my life."

"We're counting on that too." As Allen stood up, Jul had a feeling that he would hate whatever these two had up their sleeves. Instead of asking, he simply hugged Annabelle goodbye and shook Allen's hand. This might work out after all.

"You ready now?" He looked up at Sapphire when she spoke. She must have come into the office when he'd been deep in thought. "I have to get this going or Colby is going to come down on my head again. That man is driven."

"He is." Jul picked up the pictures. "Wow, these are really good. Did you take these? Or Colby?"

"Colby. I sent him and his lovely wife to France last week and had them take pictures. The children stayed with Blair and I. We had so much fun. That little Darcy is going to be a handful. But oh, so adorable."

The pictures had his full attention. They were fantastic. The first one was a close-up of a bunch of grapes. The colors were so vivid that he felt as if he could touch them. The second picture was of several different colors of grapes. The blues and greens went together so well that again, he thought it was real. But he loved the dew that hung on them, the way the sun seemed to glisten off them. He put this one to the side.

The next four were of the fields. They were good, but not all that inspiring to him. When he got to the last two, he had to lay them down. Jul stared at them, not believing what he was seeing. He looked up at Sapphire when she sat across from him.

"Where did you get this one?" He pointed to the one of his father and mother on their wedding day. It had been colored, he knew, because the original was in his home in DC, which was currently being packed up.

"Your mom told me about it and I called the movers yesterday. I didn't know where it was, but they did. Nice, isn't it?" He nodded. The picture had been taken as they exited the court house. His mom had been so shy that she'd looked at his dad rather than the camera. His dad looked as if he might burst from happiness.

Then he looked at the one of him and Emerald. It was in color as well, but someone had muted it to match the one of his parents. She was looking at him in the same manner his mom had his dad. And he, of course, had the same besotted look on his face as his dad.

"You said there were nine. I only have eight." He looked at the one with the dewy grapes, then back at the ones of Jul an Em and his parents. "I'm not sure what you have in mind here with these two, but I love this one."

She took the three pictures and then laid the ninth one in front of him. Jul knew that this was the label. Sapphire knew it too. Her grin told him that he was going to love the slogan too.

Sapphire had taken the two couples and put them on opposite sides of the label. In the middle were the grapes he'd liked. There were bottles of wine nearby, not in color, but a suggestion of what they might have within them. And under it was his last name. Simply Whitney.

"What's the name?" He looked up at her when she didn't say anything, but handed him a small piece of foil, like the kind that he used to seal around the cork. There were wolves chasing one another all along the edges. When she handed him the next artwork, he had to smile. Damn, but she was good.

"*Vins de la Lune*, or in English, Wines of the Wolf. We could put a translation on the foil, but I don't think that will be necessary." He stared at the finished product. "The color will make people pause to look at the label, and that's what we want. Most buy by the type of wine they like, then the label. Once we have them hooked that way, the rest will be easy."

"And I have you something you're going to love." He looked up at Thad when he came into the office. "I've been thinking for a few weeks now on how to do your crackers. And then I was playing with Carter, and it hit me. It had to nest."

The round cracker container landed in front of him, and he loved it. Sapphire picked it up and slipped the opening over the top of the bottle he had on his desk. It was perfect. The sections, one of crackers and the next with cheese, circled the neck as if it had been made for it. Which, he was pretty sure, it had been.

"It's made for convenience. You can slip the container over the neck and walk with the glasses in your other hand. I've played around with it for the past few days, and the crackers don't get smashed up like the ones would in a basket." Thad picked up the bottle with the cheese and showed him how well it stayed. "See? No issues of it falling off."

"You're going to give a code online when a person buys the bottle of wine that will give the person a percentage off the container. Once they start getting them together, we'll close that part off and lower the price of the wine to compensate. Not much, but a few bucks." Blair moved around the room until he too was seated at the large conference table. "You're overwhelmed again, aren't you?"

"No. On the contrary, I'm impressed." Blair grinned. "Your wife is very good at what she does."

The low growl had him laughing. Blair laughed as well as he told him what else they had planned to shoot the wine he was making out of the ball park. Jul listened intently, knowing that whatever they had in mind, he was game. This was going to be perfect, he just knew it.

~~~

Emerald was putting the last of her books on her shelf when Dawn came into the room. She'd been helping her set up her office all week, and now that they were nearly finished, she just wanted to sit back and enjoy it. Looking around, she had to smile. It was better than she'd thought.

"I have nine messages for you about teachers. I'm having background checks run on them now. Did you know that Sloan had a firm that does it better than the government?" She nodded and smiled. "It's scary what that man can do. Anyway, here are the ones that he's looking at now, and these are fails. What do you want me to do with them?"

"File them. We have to keep them for so long before we can toss them out. Did he give you the paperwork on why we are rejecting them?" Dawn nodded and told her they were in the files. "And the ones that you're running now, any of them stand out?"

"Two. One I would hire even if I just had her here as someone who could run the office. Damn, but she is organized. I read over her employer recommendations, and he said she kept him sane for the better part of ten years. But I can't find why she's leaving." Emerald nodded and watched while Dawn sorted through the files. "This one is amazing. She's leaving her pack behind because it holds too many memories. Her mate was killed a few months ago when a hunter mistook him for a wolf that was poaching on his land. She has no children, but has been a teacher for five years. Kindergarten. I've actually spoken to her and she is sort of laid back, nice, and seems to care a great deal about what sort of person you are."

"When her results come back let me know." Dawn started out of the room, and Emerald called her back. "I wanted to ask you about when you were changed. I'm sort of nervous about converting Jul."

"You really want my advice?" Emerald nodded. "Then have Blair do it. He's stronger than you. And not nearly as close to Jul as you are. When Colby did mine it was fine and all, but...well, he took it really hard that he had to hurt me. I mean really hard. I'm not saying you're not strong enough to do it. But you could support him while it's happening."

"I'm terrified of killing him." Dawn sat down and rubbed her belly while she nodded. "What if I'm not able to do it? That's my biggest fear. That my wolf would want to quit before it's complete."

"She won't do that." Emerald wasn't sure if she would or not and said as much. "This is a big deal, I get it. You're afraid, I understand that as well. But what I don't understand, if you want the truth again, is why you, this big bad wolf, is afraid? I mean, have you heard yourself when you're barking orders? You are right on top of things. Organized…just look at this school. All you have to worry about is the teachers and the students. I mean, there is more, but not the building being finished on time…which you made happen a full two weeks before the contractors said. The desks, yes, you might have something to do with those too, but you got them here on time and under budget. A wimp could not have done that."

"It's for the kids." Dawn smiled and nodded. "It's not the same as biting a man you love until he's nearly dead, and hoping that he'll live through it."

"Why not? I mean, it's life or death here too. If a person tried to get in here to harm anyone of the children or people who worked here, what do you think would happen?"

"I'd kill them." Dawn nodded and stood this time. "I'd kill them. My wolf would come out and she'd fucking kill them."

"Exactly. And you're going to be no less brave for what is going to happen tonight. She's going to know it's her mate and that if she screws up, then he's as good as dead." Dawn snapped her fingers on Emerald's head as she walked by. "Stop thinking so hard. It's going to be great. And I'm going to be there cheering you all on. Maybe."

"Maybe?" Dawn nodded and nearly doubled over. "Shit. Are you in labor? Why didn't you say something?"

"I wanted to make sure the office was set up before I had to leave." Emerald reached for Ruby and Diamond. Dawn kept talking, but it was labored now, pants of air accompanying each word. "I don't think we're going to make it anywhere soon. Colby is coming now, and he's bringing…oh Emerald. I'm ready."

"Ready?" Dawn nodded as she lay down on the floor. "Ready for what? Not to have this kid! You can't have it now. I'm...I have no idea what to do. Tell me you're kidding."

The scream tore through the room and Emerald wanted to scream as well. The baby was coming, and she was there alone. Christ. She reached for Jul just as Dawn told her it was time right now.

*She's having the baby. Dawn is having the baby.* He told her he was on his way. *It might be too late.*

*I'm on my way.*

When Dawn screamed again, this time bent nearly in half telling Emerald to help her, Emerald took a deep breath and let her wolf guide her. As soon as she saw the baby's head, Emerald knew she could do anything after this.

# Chapter 12

The gathering was full tonight. Blair looked out over his pack and had to smile. Who would have thought that he'd be the alpha of so many people? Hell, he didn't believe it either. When Sapphire put her arms around him from behind, he lifted her hand and kissed it before turning her into his arms.

"There is very little food left, so your grandmother is sending out some of the pack for pizzas. I think they have been starving themselves for this." Sapphire laughed and held onto him as he continued. "Have you talked to Em yet?" They'd all taken to calling her Em since Jul had come into their family. It suited her.

"Twice. She just threw me out of her room. I think that this is going to go very well tonight. Both of them seemed to be very calm when I left them." Blair had thought so too, but Sapphire knew her sister better than he did. "I don't think they'll have any problems."

He hoped not. Blair really liked Jul. He was calming and smart. There were times here lately that he'd gone by his office just to sit and talk about really nothing at all. And

Jul had never been upset about him just showing up. Blair wanted this to work in the worst sort of way.

"We're ready." He turned to look at Jul and Em when she spoke. "Jul understands what he has to do, and we're to let you do the introductions. I think that's what we're supposed to do, right?" Blair nodded.

When they left the shelter, a silence settled over the several hundred others that made him think of a volume being turned down in small degrees. As soon as Em came out with Jul and Sapphire, everyone cheered. This was her night.

"Tonight we're going to welcome Julius Whitney into our pack. Emerald Whitney, his wife, will convert him in the ways of our kind." Applause broke out, but it was over quickly. "When the ceremony begins, please be careful not to distract them. This is, as some of you know, a very dangerous and scary process. Please be considerate of them."

As soon as he nodded, Jul stepped forward. He'd been told all the things that were to happen several times, and when he tossed off his robe and danced around the circle naked, everyone laughed. The man was taking this very well. When Em stepped up beside him, Jul helped her pull her own robe off, and then he kissed her. It was not passionate, but one of love. As soon as she stepped back, Em let her wolf take her.

The large stone that had been in the center of the circle since he'd taken the pack over was covered in a dark material. It wasn't anything that had to be there, but since it was coming up on winter he'd opted for it to be covered so it wouldn't be so cold. As Jul lay over it, he looked over at him.

*You'll help her if she needs it.* Blair nodded. *She won't, but you be there in the event something happens. Don't let her die.*

*I won't. I promise.* Jul nodded this time and looked at Em. Her wolf was standing near the dais as she waited on him to proceed. Blair was very nervous himself. A lot of things could go wrong.

"You ready, honey?" Em nodded at him, and Blair realized how much her wolf had changed in the last weeks. She was thicker, her fur was fuller, and she no longer looked haunted. He realized then that she was happy.

As soon as he nodded to her, she lunged at Jul. The bite to his belly was harsh, and needed to be done in a way that she'd taste not just his blood, but his bowel too. Jul only moved once and settled down almost immediately. He never made a sound when she tore viciously into his body.

Time seemed to slow down for Blair as he monitored Jul. His heart rate had picked up a great deal when she bit into him, but had settled quickly. Now, twenty minutes later, it was starting to slow more. He looked at Em as she held her powerful jaws around Jul.

In another ten minutes his heart rate was barely audible, and his breathing was slowing as well. Em growled at him when he reached over to pet her, and Blair backed off. He should know better than to do that, but he needed comforting. When Jul put his hand up and settled it over Em's head, she whimpered a little but didn't move. It was time for her to do the most damage.

The big wolf growled and tore into his flesh again. This time Jul screamed, but he didn't move. As Em held onto him, she climbed up on the big stone and lay her body over him. It was then that Blair thought the big man wasn't going to make it.

His heart rate dropped again. He had to listen hard to hear it, and when he put his fingers to his throat to check, he couldn't feel it at all. Blair called for Sloan to step in. As he moved to open his wrist, Em spoke to him.

*He's not going to die.* Blair started to tell her what he could hear and not hear. *You touch him and I will tear you apart, Blair. I don't care what you think. He will not die by my hand.*

"You can hear his heart as well as I can. He's dying, Em. You told me to step in if things got—"

*You touch him, either of you, and I will tear out your throat. I have this. He's going to live.* She growled again when he decided the best way to handle this was to shift and take her down, but she told him again that she'd kill him. And right now, he believed her.

"Listen." He looked over at Sloan when he spoke. "Christ, he's getting stronger. Listen to his heart, Blair. The fucker is going to make it."

It was getting stronger. And when Em looked up at him, her eyes full of happiness, he also knew she was as well. Blair reached out carefully and ran his fingers through her fur. Then they turned to the crowd.

"Our newest pack member." The crowd went wild. Those that weren't wolves already shifted and ran around with their own mates. The children came running up to the dais and threw bouquets of flowers at the couple.

Sapphire came to stand beside Blair. "She would have killed you." He nodded. "Next time you get the urge to piss off one of my sisters, can you please make sure that I don't have a front-row seat? I was ready to help her."

"I love you too." Blair kissed his mate on the nose as he moved back for the well-wishers. "I have to tell you something. Em is far and away the bravest wolf or human I've ever met. I don't think...hell, I know that I would never have been able to do what she just did. Changing a mate...anyone...has got to be the hardest thing I've ever witnessed."

Sapphire squeezed him to her, and he looked down. There were tear stains on her cheeks, and he could see how relieved she was. He was as well. Blair never wanted to go through this again.

~~~

Jul woke but didn't open his eyes. It was hard enough just trying to think, much less try to see. When he heard what he swore was a bug walking on the wall, he opened one eye and looked around. Blair was sitting in the chair next to him, and Em was curled up in the other chair. Both of them appeared to be sleeping.

Sitting up slightly, he was shoved back down by a firm hand. Looking to his right, he looked into the laughing face of Allen. As he sat back down, Jul lay back too. Just that little movement had exhausted him.

*Come out better than we thought.* Jul nodded. He wasn't sure what that meant, but he was glad to know that he'd made it. *Let them sleep a bit. I'd like to talk to you a little while if you don't mind.*

*No. I'm assuming that since I'm in this pack, I can talk to everyone this way.* Allen nodded. *Will everyone be able to hear us?*

*Not unless you invite them. What I have to say I'd rather you didn't.* Jul nodded again. *It's about that mom of yours. I wanted to ask you if you mind much if I took her out.*

*My mom?* Allen laughed and said yeah. *You want to date my mom? I don't understand. She's my mom.*

*Yeah, boy, I got that. She's your mom. But she's a right fine woman and she...well, I'd like to take her out once in a while. We done sort of hit it off. Not like she's my mate or anything, but...well, to tell you the truth of the matter, I'm sort of sweet on her.*

*My mom?* Allen said if he said that again he was going to hit him. *Allen, please forgive me, but I don't know why you're asking me. I mean, she's my mom, not my daughter.*

*Don't you think I know that?* Allen scrubbed his hand over his face before continuing, *She's special. I don't want to kid around with her like I do other women. I want to treat her with respect, like...well, like the wonderful woman that she is.*

*She is very special.* Allen nodded, and Jul could see that the older man really was smitten with his mom. *But why are you asking me and not her? I would think that would be who you'd be wanting to get permission from.*

*You're her son. Her only child, right?* Jul nodded, feeling like he'd been put in one of those places where they punked you or something. *As her son, I'm asking you because it's you she'll worry about. I'm not saying that I want to have sex with her, or —*

*And if you do, please, for Christ's sake, don't tell me.* Allen laughed and nodded. *I understand that you feel the need to ask me, but, ultimately, it's my mom that's going to decide. I mean, Dad has been gone for ten years now. I know she's been out, but nothing serious. I don't think she's looking for serious.*

*I'm not either. Just a good time with a lovely lady.* Jul wanted to ask him how good a time, but didn't. There were some things a son just did not want to know. *I'd be respectful of her and you. I'd never do anything to cause her harm, or to have you pissy with me.*

Something moved along his skin, and he looked at his arm. Allen laughed again, and then told him he needed to get his strength up before letting his wolf come out to play.

"I'm a wolf." Allen nodded and leaned back in his chair. "Holy shit, Allen. I'm a fucking wolf."

"You know, you repeat yourself a lot. Why do you do that? Some sort of ailment?" Jul sat up. His entire body felt energized right now. "Calm him down. Tell him things are all right."

"Jul." He looked at Em, and he wanted her. Not soon, but right now. The low growl that escaped from him had her standing up, but she didn't move. Blair stood as well, but when he moved to stand in front of Em, Jul growled again.

"Jul, you're not strong enough to shift yet." Jul felt like he could take on the world despite what Blair was saying. "Calm your wolf before you get hurt."

Never taking his eyes from Em, he told the other two men to get out. Blair started to speak, but Allen told him it was right as rain, whatever the hell that meant. As soon as the door closed behind them, Jul sat up with his feet on the side of the bed now.

"I want you." Em nodded but still hadn't moved. "Strip for me. Right now, before I do it for you. I need to fuck you."

"Your wolf wants to mark me." Jul nodded. "He's going to take you if you don't calm him down. And you are very weak from what happened last night."

"Take off your clothes, Em, or I will." He felt the wolf run along his body again. "Christ, he wants you."

The wolf took him. He knew the exact moment when he went from human to wolf, and moaned at the feeling. Every part of him wanted to run, leap into the air, but he needed to have Em more. When she started to pull her clothing off, he got off the bed and moved around her. Her scent, the smell that he knew was her arousal, was making him wild to have her.

*He needs to taste you. Can he do that? Lick you until you…Christ, Em, he wants to eat you.* Em moaned, and her powerful scent nearly had him taking her to the floor. *Hurry.*

She was naked before him when he circled her again. The thought of taking her wolf had his own panting with need. But for right now he wanted to eat her pussy. He told her to lay on the bed, and she did it quickly. Jul moved to stand between her spread legs and raised his muzzle to the air to get more of her inside of him. When she moaned again, her legs trembled and he knew that he couldn't wait any longer. Burying his nose into her curls, Jul knew what real paradise was.

His tongue felt different to him, thicker and longer. He lapped at her several times before he realized he could fuck her this way. Moving his tongue into her sheath, he nearly came when he tasted her. Every part of her was different to him.

Her first climax had his wolf growling as he lapped greedily at her. Jul thought for sure that he was going to catch hell for this, but she curled her hand into his fur and held him tightly to her as she rode his mouth. The thought of sinking his teeth into her was both arousing and frightening.

"Lick my thigh. Then when I come again, bite me. It'll seal the bond." Jul wanted to tell her he couldn't hurt her, but she spread her legs wider and he licked her clit until she came again. His wolf had no such problems with biting her, and after licking her inner thigh, he bit into her hard enough that Jul tasted blood. Her scream had him tearing at her flesh. The mark, the bite-like scar, formed almost as soon as he let her go. Jul watched as she slid her fingers into her pussy and began riding her own fingers. "Fuck me, Jul. Please?"

Jul felt the wolf curl back into him. His hands, which still held Em open, were human now, and his mouth, before full of sharp canines, was again his own. Pulling her nether lips wider open, he suckled at her clit until she came twice more. She was his, all his, and he had to have all of her. Fisting his cock, he stood up over her. Christ, his cock was so painful that he was sure he'd come as soon as he entered her.

"Fuck me." He nodded at her demand, and when she sat up and took him into her mouth, Jul threw back his head and felt his eyes roll to the back of his head. His balls were tight to his body, his cock so stretched that he knew that if he got any harder he was going to hurt. But when she lay back, her body spread out like a feast for him, he moved over her, guiding his cock into her. When he was seated as far as he could go, he paused to look down at her.

"I love you." She grinned at him and wrapped her legs over his. "Christ, do you have any idea how delicious you taste to us? How much the thought of running with you in the woods is making us crazy?"

"Yes." He laughed and moved out of her slowly, then back into her. "I need you to fuck me. Take me hard and fill me with your seed."

His cock seemed to leap hard into her, and she cried out, not from pain but from pleasure. As he began to pound into her, taking her as hard as he could, she dug her nails into his back and held him to her. Jul felt her tongue make a wet, hot path down his throat, and when she came, her body tightening around his, she sank her teeth into his shoulder and brought him over the edge. Jul bit into her as well, tearing into her flesh until he tasted her hot, spicy blood filling his mouth. Jul's world began to shift beneath him, his vision darkened, and he felt himself slipping away as his mate, his true love, screamed out his name again and again.

When he woke again, Em was curled around him. There was a blanket over the two of them too. Stretching just enough to feel his body but not enough to wake her, he thought about what had happened to him.

A wolf. He was a wolf. Smiling, he wondered what other wonderful and amazing things he could do now, and thought about the conversation he'd had with Quentin just a few days ago. The man knew a lot about what he would be feeling.

"Don't take things too quickly." That was Quentin's first bit of advice, and when Em moved her hand over his cock, Jul knew that one had fallen by the wayside. His second pearl of wisdom had been to make sure that he ate a lot of meat. It would give him the strength he'd need to handle all the changes in his body. Jul made a mental note to tell Curtis to have more red meat in the meals for a while. The next thing was to make sure that he formed a connection to the other members of the family. He'd already figured out that Allen and he had a connection, and wondered who else. Reaching for Quentin, he was surprised to feel the man connect so quickly.

*It's doubtful that you're going to do anything by small measures, are you?* He asked him what he meant. *Usually the new wolf waits for a week or so before showing. You might have a little trouble controlling him, but you seemed to have gotten the hang of that. Then there was your conversion. We all thought you were dead, buddy.*

*Dead?* Quentin told him how close it had been. *But she saved me. Em converted me and saved my life.*

*That she did. Nearly had to kill Blair to keep him from bringing Sloan in too.* Quentin laughed again. *You have yourself one hell of a mate there. And I'm proud to call you my brother.*

*I am as well.* When the connection was closed, he thought about Em. She'd done it. No matter what the odds had been against them, she'd done it. Pulling her closer to his body, he saw her look up at him and smile.

"Hello." He kissed her gently on the mouth and told her he loved her. "And I love you as well. You are doing really well now. How do you feel?"

"Like I'm the biggest, baddest wolf around, and have the most gorgeous mate a man would ever want." She giggled, and he smiled. "When can we go home? I know this is Blair's house, but I want us to be alone in our own home."

"Noelle will be coming tomorrow." She looked nervous, and he kissed her again. "Are you sure about this? I mean, I want her to be ours, but are you sure?"

"Yes. We'll have a daughter to raise, and someday, children of our own." She nodded and smiled up at him. "You do want children, don't you?"

"Yes. I want all you can give me." He rolled her to her back and slid deep inside of her. "I thought you wanted to go home."

"I do. But I need to take you again." He moved slowly, feeling each tightening of her sheath as he moved in and out of her. "You're so tight around me. Milking my cock like you did with your mouth."

"I need to come." He nodded, but continued to move slowly. "Jul, please. Finish me so I can scream out your name."

"I will." He was feeling the burn to do what she wanted. His balls, full again, needed relief. When she moaned, Jul felt it with his entire being. And when she rolled her hips up to meet his, he knew he wasn't going to last much longer. "Come for me, love. Come now."

She threw back her head and held him as her climax rolled out of her. Watching her, mesmerized by her, his own climax took his breath away when it took him. Holding her tightly as he emptied into her, all Jul could think about was filling her with his child. He dropped onto her and felt sleep take him again.

Over an hour later, he was holding her to him. Then he asked her when they could start on a child. Her grin made him want to throw her back to the bed and take her again and again. But she got up and started to pull on clothes before she answered.

"I'd like to have one soon, but I'm not in heat right now." He remembered someone telling him about that. "But before we have a baby, we have to get some things straight. I'm not going to quit my job to be a stay-at-home mom. I want to work too."

"All right." She turned to look at him. "I have no problem being a stay-at-home dad. In fact, with the building underway right now, by the time we do have a baby, I should have things well under control everywhere, and can be here more than at a job site."

"You don't mind?" He shook his head and wondered what else was on her mind. "I would like to...there are several children that I'd like to consider taking into our home as well. Most of them are...not all of them are wolf. One is a cat."

"Adoption, you mean?" She nodded. "I'm not opposed to that either. We have the means to give a child all we can. And if we don't, then we'll help find them somewhere safe. I want you to be happy, and if this does it, then—"

"We'd be parents of other people's children. Raised by us. They'd need both of us." Jul watched her. There was something wrong here, and he couldn't figure it out. Then it hit him.

"You're worried about another child coming to you, aren't you? You're afraid that another child will be hurt, and there will be nothing you can do about it." She nodded, and he got up to hold her. "We'll do everything we can, love. I promise you that. No matter if I end up in jail, we'll not let another child be hurt that way."

"I can't fail again." He held her while she cried and thought about finding where Sloan had taken those parents and digging them up to kill them again. "He needed me and I failed him."

"You didn't fail anyone. His parents did. And now that we can do something to help other children, we will." He lifted her chin up so he could see her eyes. "I promise you. So long as we're alive, no child we know will suffer like that again. Okay?"

At her nod, he pulled her back into his arms. He would do everything within his power to make sure that he kept his promise to her too. Even if, like he said, he had to go to jail.

# Chapter 13

Three years later

"I'm not going to throw up." Allen looked at his future son and growled at him again. "I swear to you, if you tell me once again to calm down, I'm going to show you calm. I'm calm, damn it."

"Of course you are." Jul jumped back when he swiped at him. "If you shift now, Mom is going to be really pissed at you. She said that this is the last time this is going to happen."

"That wasn't my fault." Allen knew it wasn't, and he was pretty sure that everyone else did too. It wasn't his fault that his wolf had gotten the better of him when he'd been in his other tux. And damn it, that had been six months ago. Couldn't a man have a minute of peace when he messed up? When Blair walked into the little room, Allen thought he had an ally and glared at Jul.

"Celeste said to tell you if you tear this tux, she's moving back to DC and never speaking to you again." So much for his own son helping him out. "She also looks like an angel."

"Of course she does." Allen got up to pace and calm his stupid wolf. Who knew that at his age he'd be getting married again? And to someone like Celeste Whitney? She wasn't his mate, no, but he loved her with all his heart. "How much longer we gonna be cooped up in this oven?"

"Ten minutes. The girls are still working on getting dressed. You should also know that when this is over, Sapphire and I are going to leave." Allen glared at his son and asked him why. "She's in labor."

"Hot damn, another grandbaby." He nearly told him to take her now, but he knew as surely as he was sitting there neither of them would be leaving him. Allen loved Sapphire as much, if not sometimes more than, he did his own flesh and blood. "She doing okay today?"

Blair nodded. All of them missed Annabelle. She'd been gone nearly a year now, and sometimes the pain of it hit him hard. He wasn't sure how those girls of hers did it every day, knowing that she was lost to them too.

She'd been out in the garden with Allen. They'd been picking green beans, the last of them of the season, when she'd told him she needed to sit down. It had scared him something terrible, because she never sat down unless all the work was done. When she seemed to have collapsed where she stood, he sat down beside her, knowing somehow that this was the end.

"Them girls can be right here." She shook her head and smiled at him. He could see her pain then, and wanted to pick her up and carry her to the house.

"No, please don't. This is where I want to be. And with you." He nodded as the tears started to flow from his eyes. "You're my best friend, did you know that? No one in this world has come to mean more to me as a friend than you have."

"I love you too. You old bat, are you gonna die on me?" She nodded and closed her eyes, but her smile was right there. "Don't you do it. I need them girls here so you can tell them your goodbyes."

"You tell them for me." Her voice was weaker, but she'd looked at him. "I need to tell you a few things before I go to be with my mate. It's about them girls. You tell them that I loved them like my own children, and raising them up was a pleasure, never a hardship."

"I'll do that." He thought about reaching for them then, but knew that if he did, not a one of them would have made it to her. And he also knew that he couldn't have gone against her wishes.

"Do you love Celeste?" Allen nodded before he thought about what he was saying. "I knew you did. Marry her. Make her happy for me."

"You gonna make all these demands? If so, then maybe I should go and get me some paper to write it down." He held her hand when she put it in his. "Don't leave me, Annabelle. I won't know what to do without you."

"You'll flirt with every skirt you see and put the tomatoes too close together." He smiled because he knew that he'd do just that. "I need to lay back now."

He helped her to lay in the dirt she loved so well. The beans they'd pulled up, all the empty bushes, were haloed around her like a wreath. He sat beside her while her breathing slowed and her eyes closed for longer periods of time.

"Allen? Tell Sapphire that she's to name her little girl for me. I'm an old woman and need to have that in my after life." He nodded. "And tell Diamond to be what she wants. Go back to school and become the administrator of that hospital, and kick Josh to the curb. He has his own work to care for."

"I'll do that." He wiped at the tears again. "I should call them girls, Annabelle. They should be here with you."

"Jade will need the most loving after I'm gone. She's strong, but she's tender. Tell her I thought of her often." Allen held her hand tightly when she stopped breathing for a few moments. His own heart had skipped a few beats as well. "Tell Opal to shine. She'll know what to do."

Annabelle laid there for several minutes after that. He'd held her hand as it grew colder and colder. When she opened her eyes and looked at him, Allen would have sworn that she wasn't seeing him, but beyond him. Then she spoke of her last two granddaughters.

"I don't have much time left. He's coming for me." Allen nodded. "Tell Ruby that the baby will be fine if she only lets her have her own feet. And the next girls will be no different, I think. That little one will run her ragged if she tries to hold her in much longer. And Emerald, my little beautiful Em. She will love those babies like they're her own, won't she?"

"Yes. She and Jul have helped so many little ones. She's a wonderful mom." There had been no children for the couple of their own. Em had never gone into heat once since she and Jul had become mates. Everyone worried, and there was a sadness around the poor girl that no one could help her with.

"She's going to have a set of twins. Tell her that for me. Tell her that her twins will be with her soon." Allen cried harder when his Annabelle let go of his hand. But still he'd held her, even when she didn't speak to him again. It wasn't until then that he'd called Blair to tell him.

"Dad?" Allen looked up at his son. "You okay? You sort of spaced out there for a moment."

"I'm fine. Remembering a fine lady is all I was doing." Blair nodded and smiled at him. "She would have been crowing to the world today, wouldn't she?"

"She would at that. And how right she'd been about everything." Allen nodded and stood up. "I have something for you. I wanted...Sapphire and the girls thought you'd like to have this today."

When Blair walked away, Jul came to stand in front of him. The boy had turned out all right, and now that his little Em was going to have those twins soon, the boy was about to bust with happiness.

"She's here with us, I think." Allen nodded, knowing that he was right. "She was one very special lady."

"I know."

When Blair handed him a small box, he was almost afraid to open it. But when he did, he had to sit down again, the overwhelming grief and happiness taking his breath away.

"You and them made this for me?" Blair nodded his head as he pulled out the small pendant that Sapphire had had made. "Damn, but them girls are going to make me all soggy on my wedding day. See that they don't."

As Blair helped him pin it to his tux, Allen knew as surely as he was standing there that this thing would be the first thing he put on in the morning and the last thing he took off. When Blair stepped back, he walked to the mirror and looked at it.

The long green bean was perfect. At about three inches long and about as wide as his finger, it stuck out like a sore thumb. But it was just what he needed, everything he needed to give him the courage to go through this today.

"I loved her, you know. Not like I do my Celeste, but just about as close as a man could love a woman he thought of as his mom." Blair told him they all knew that. "I miss her more than I do my own mother some days. She was a damn sight more loving than mine was."

"Annabelle loved you too. And I think perhaps she's looking down on us all today." Allen was sure of it as he turned to his son. "Dad, I'm very proud of you and love you with all my heart. I can't...don't leave me. Okay? I don't think I could stand it if you did."

"I'm going to try my best, boy, but I got places I might want to go someday, and you can't be coming along with me." Blair nodded and pulled him in for a hard hug. "I love you, son. More than I tell you every day, I love you."

As they got their things together and waited for someone to tell him it was time, Allen looked at the two men he would call his sons. Neither of them knew the depth of his love for them, and both men were in his heart deeper than anyone he knew. Even Jul, a son that was not his blood, was the world to him. His favorite boy of all the gems.

"Ready?" He nodded when Blair told him it was time. "You're going to make her very happy, Dad. I know it."

"Hell, boy, she's already made me the happiest man in this here world. Her saying she'd be my wife was the best thing that could happen to me." Allen moved up to the dais and looked around at his family. All of them. "Yes, sir, I'm the happiest man in the world right now."

~~~

Blair held his daughter while Sapphire moved around the room making sure that everyone had everything they needed. He was pretty sure she knew that they could get everything on their own, but he loved watching her. When his daughter stirred in his arms, he looked at Carter, who was sitting next to him.

"Dad, she gonna cry again?" Blair told him he didn't know. "She sure is loud when she don't get her way. Is she always going to be that way?"

"I would say that's a good bet." Carter rolled his eyes. "What if I told you that you were the same way when you were her age? What do you think of that?"

"I was not, and if I was, you should have thrown me to the alligators." He glanced up at Jade when his son grinned at him. "Aunt Jade said that that's what you did to all the other kids that you and Mom had that were bad."

"Daddy's going to beat your Aunt Jade's butt when we get alone." Carter laughed, and Jade turned to look at them. Her smile made him think she knew they were talking about her. "She's only kidding; you know that, don't you, son?"

"Yeah, I know it." He watched his sister as she settled back down. "Dad, do you think I could have a brother? I know we have to keep this one, but can you please put in an order for me a brother?"

"I'll talk to your mother." He switched arms and held Annabelle while Carter squirmed around. "Would you hold her for me for a minute? I'd like to get me a drink of water."

Carter looked at him as if he was waiting for the punchline. Instead, Blair moved the baby around so that he could cradle her in Carter's arms. Annabelle was almost six months old and just about the most precious thing in the world to him, but Carter didn't care much for her, and Blair thought maybe if he held her, he might change his mind.

When he had her in his arms and Blair had given him a few pointers, like not to drop her and please don't squeeze her too tightly, he got up. Walking away from his children was the hardest thing he'd ever done so far as a parent. When Sapphire looked at him, then at the kids, he watched her turn her back on them as well. Damn, but he loved his wife.

Blair took his time getting a bottle of water. He never really looked back, just a few glances to let him know that they were still in one piece, but he did have a couple of people he was talking to look for him. After ten minutes he made his way back to them. Carter was talking to his now awake sister.

"She's all right. The one you have to watch out for is Aunt Jade. She's a pistol. You'll really like Aunt Opal. She makes all kinds of stuff to make Momma happy. That thing in your hair too. She made that." Carter touched it with his fingers. "It's real girly, but it looks okay on you."

"You giving her the scoop?" He nodded, and Blair sat down. Annabelle never took her eyes off her brother as he continued. Blair had to look away. He'd never felt such pride for someone before.

"And Aunt Em? Man, she is the coolest. You don't know it yet, but she takes in kids that nobody wants. And next month she and Uncle Jul are going to have two of their own. I can't wait." Annabelle jabbered something at him, and Carter nodded. "You said it. Twins. I love all the kids. Some of them are older than me, like Noelle, but she's had a hard life, Aunt Em told me. But she's really smart, and sometimes she tells me she talks to her brother."

Blair started to ask him what he'd said, but Annabelle started talking again. And this time he was sure that Carter understood her. When she finished, Blair turned to his son and asked him about it.

"Yeah, sure. If you listen to her. I hear her all the time and go into her room to read to her when she can't sleep." Blair looked for Sapphire, and when she looked at him, he told her to come here. "Sometimes Great Grams is there too."

"You talk to Annabelle, Mom's grandmother?" He nodded as if that was the most natural thing in the world. He told Sapphire what he'd said, and she smiled.

"Is she doing okay?" Blair wanted to tell his mate not to encourage such behavior, but Carter answered her before he could.

"She's doing great. I'm supposed to tell you that Aunt Em isn't the only one that is having twins. What does that mean?" Blair looked at Sapphire's flat belly, then at his son. They were expecting, and no one knew it as yet. They were holding it to their own hearts until later. "Am I gonna have some more sisters? I'd really like to have a brother or two. Anna is great, but…sheesh, are you crying again?"

Sapphire stood up and went to the bathroom. She'd been doing that a lot lately, and he knew why. She missed her grandmother. And now with his dad being married, it was bringing it all home again. Dad had been with her when she'd passed, and Sapphire felt closer to him for that.

After the dinner was over, Blair and his dad went out to the deck. The other men were out there, but he moved to the corner where they could be alone. His dad spoke before he could ask him what he wanted.

"I know that you and Sapphire are breeding again. I'm so happy for you, son." He nodded and watched as Thad and Jul played catch with his son. "I guess you'll be wanting us to move out."

"No." His dad looked at him, and Blair realized how loud he'd been. "Please don't leave us. Sapphire has been upset for days thinking you'd want your own place. And she and Celeste have been bawling over the dumbest things to take out of here. If you leave here and take Celeste, I think it'll be like losing her grandmother all over."

"I don't want to go." His dad looked over at the garden, at rest now at the end of the season. "I still plant the tomatoes too close, and I can't get a straight row to save my life. If I leave here…well, hell son, I don't want to go. I'm having too much fun with that boy of yours. Did you know that he talks to her?"

"He just told me. And I think he talks to Annabelle, the baby, too." His dad nodded, still staring at the garden. "Dad, please don't leave us. We need you."

"I'm not going nowhere. I'm here for as long and you'll have me."

Blair did something he'd not done in years. He pulled his dad to him and hugged him. Tears threatened again, and he let them go. He didn't even care that his entire family saw him. Blair knew as surely as he was standing there that nothing would come between him and his family.

## Before You Go...

Share your voice and help guide other readers to these wonderful books. Even if it's only a line or two your reviews help readers discover the author's books so they can continue creating stories that you'll love. Login to your favorite retailer and leave a review. Thank you.

AWARD WINNING, BESTSELLING AUTHOR

Kathi Barton, author of the bestselling series Force of Nature, lives in Nashport, Ohio with her husband Paul. In addition to writing full time Kathi likes to spend time with her eight grandkids, three children and three children-in-laws. She writes to relax and have fun.

Her muse, a cross between Jimmy Stewart and Hugh Jackman brings them to life for her readers in a way that has them coming back time and again for more. Her favorite genre is paranormal romance with a great deal of spice. You can visit Kathi on line and drop her an email if you'd like. She loves hearing from her fans. aaronskiss@gmail.com.

Follow Kathi on her blog:
http://kathisbartonauthor.blogspot.com/